Ziggy and the

the

#6

Black Dinosaurs

Stars and Sparks on Stage

By Sharon M. Draper
Illustrated by Jesse Joshua Watson

Aladdin Paperbacks
New York London Toronto Sydney

❧

ALADDIN PAPERBACKS
An imprint of Simon & Schuster Children's Publishing Division
1230 Avenue of the Americas, New York, NY 10020
Text copyright © 2007 by Sharon M. Draper
Illustrations copyright © 2007 by Jesse Joshua Watson
All rights reserved, including the right of reproduction in whole or in part in any form.
ALADDIN PAPERBACKS and colophon are trademarks of Simon & Schuster, Inc.
Designed by Lisa Vega
The text of this book was set in Minion.
Manufactured in the United States of America
First Aladdin Paperbacks edition January 2007
2 4 6 8 10 9 7 5 3
The Library of Congress Control Number for the library edition is 2006931997.
ISBN-13: 978-1-4169-0001-6 (pbk)
ISBN-10: 1-4169-0001-2 (pbk)
ISBN-13: 978-1-4169-2755-6 (library)
ISBN-10: 1-4169-2755-7 (library)

This book is dedicated to
Crystal Draper and Kenyon Adams,
two genuine stars who are sparks on any stage.

Stars and Sparks on Stage

One

Ziggy's bathroom, hot and steamy from the torrent of water that poured into his shower, was filled with mist and music. Ziggy's enthusiastically loud singing voice echoed through the room. He sang as much as he could remember of "On Top of Old Smoky" while he lathered himself with his favorite shower gel. It smelled like grapes. While he rinsed off, he sang several verses of "My Darling Clementine."

"IN A CAVERN, IN A CANYON,
EXCAVATING FOR A MINE,

LIVED A MINER, FORTY-NINER

AND HIS DAUGHTER CLEMENTINE.

OH MY DARLING, OH MY DARLING,

OH MY DARLING CLEMENTINE!

YOU ARE LOST AND GONE FOREVER,

DREADFUL SORRY, CLEMENTINE!"

As he toweled himself dry, he wondered who Clementine was and what had happened to her, marveling how the words to songs sometimes didn't make much sense. He got himself dressed for school, choosing a bright red T-shirt and purple cut-off shorts. He continued to sing, this time trying out his favorite Jamaican folk song. He always sang his own crazy version of the popular words.

"DAY-O, DAY-O,

DAYLIGHT COME AND ME WANNA GO

  HOME.

DAY-O, DAY-O,

Daylight come and me wanna go
home.
Come Mr. Silly Man, peel me a
banana.
Daylight come and me wanna go
home.
Come Mr. Silly Man, peel me a
banana.
Daylight come and me wanna go
home."

Still humming, he hurried down the stairs to the kitchen, taking two steps at a time and almost bumping into his mother.

"What be the hurry, my singin' son?" she asked as she hugged him. Ziggy and his family had moved from Jamaica to Ohio when he was a little boy.

"The tryouts for the school talent show are after school today, Mum!" Ziggy told her as he packed his lunch box with three pickles, three bananas, three soft taco shells, and a small jar of orange marmalade. "The Black Dinosaurs are going to enter the competition. First prize is two hundred dollars!"

"And what would the Black Dinosaurs be doin' with that much money?" she asked. She said nothing about his strange choices for lunch—she had long ago given up trying to understand what Ziggy liked to eat. Today it would be banana-pickle tacos covered with marmalade.

"We're gonna fix up the clubhouse! We're gonna buy a card table and some lawn chairs that aren't broken. Maybe get some paint for the walls. Carpet! Cable TV! A video game player! A computer with Internet access!" His mother rolled her eyes. "Okay, okay. You know I get carried away, Mum. But we do want to get some stuff to make it just a little bit nicer. The Black Dinosaurs deserve the best! Plus we'll have a little left over to buy CDs and stuff."

The Black Dinosaurs was the name of the club Ziggy and his friends Rashawn, Rico, and Jerome had started during one summer vacation. They had built a clubhouse in Ziggy's backyard, and they had meetings when they felt like it—usually on Saturdays during the school year. Sometimes they met just to goof off and eat pizza, and sometimes they tried to solve neighborhood mysteries.

"Don't you think you should win the competition before you start spending the money?" Ziggy's mother asked with a chuckle.

"Oh, we'll win, Mum," Ziggy said with confidence. "We'll win for sure. Didn't you just hear me singing?" He ate a cold piece of pizza and drank a cup of warm chicken soup for his breakfast.

His mother laughed out loud. "Yes, son, I heard you singing. Loud and clear. Have a great day at school, and good luck at the tryouts."

Ziggy waved good-bye and headed out the door, bursting into song once again. He headed down the street, his arms swinging beside him in rhythm with the music.

"She'll be coming 'round the
mountain when she comes.
She'll be coming 'round the
mountain when she comes.

SHE'LL BE COMING 'ROUND THE
MOUNTAIN,
SHE'LL BE COMING 'ROUND THE
MOUNTAIN,
SHE'LL BE COMING 'ROUND THE
MOUNTAIN WHEN SHE COMES."

Ziggy was so caught up in his singing that he didn't notice when Rico, Jerome, and Rashawn tiptoed behind him. They put their hands to their mouths, stifling their giggles as they followed Ziggy, imitating his every move. Ziggy continued to sing at the top of his lungs.

"SHE'LL BE WEARING RED PAJAMAS
WHEN SHE COMES.
SHE'LL BE WEARING RED PAJAMAS WHEN
SHE COMES.
SHE'LL BE WEARING RED PAJAMAS,
SHE'LL BE WEARING RED PAJAMAS,
SHE'LL BE WEARING RED PAJAMAS WHEN
SHE COMES."

"Red pajamas?" Rashawn finally said, as he bumped into Ziggy. "Who's gonna be wearing red pj's?"

"And what's her name?" Rico asked with a laugh. "Nobody knows her name! All you ever hear is *she*!"

Ziggy stopped, turned, and made a funny face, and the four friends burst into laughter. "You been followin' me? Tryin' to take notes so you can sing as good as Ziggy at the tryouts?"

"Yeah, right," Jerome said, bumping Ziggy on the other side.

The four boys lived on the same street and usually walked to school together in the morning. The school building, which was only a couple of blocks away from where the boys lived, had been built more than a hundred years ago. It was large and brown and scary-looking at night, but in the daytime the boys had decided it just looked old and tired.

"I thought we were going to sing as a group—a quartet," Rico said.

"We are," Jerome answered with excitement. "The four of us are gonna be so good at the talent show that some big-time recording dude will probably try to cut us a CD!"

"Yeah!" Rashawn added. "And offer us a million-dollar recording contract!"

"And we'll have our pictures on the cover, mon!" Ziggy said, posing as if for a camera.

"You think we ought to practice a little more for the tryouts first?" Rico asked sensibly. The boys had been practicing their singing routine for weeks now. They had added dance moves and had even talked about costumes for the show.

"Good idea, mon!" Ziggy said cheerfully. "Let's go behind the school before the bell rings and make sure we've got our act together. We don't want anyone to copy our moves!"

The boys ran eagerly toward the school, all four of them loudly singing more crazy verses to "She'll be Coming 'Round the Mountain." Ziggy started out, and the other three boys joined in.

"She'll be eating French-fried
    carrots when she comes.
She'll be eating French-fried
    carrots when she comes.
She'll be eating French-fried
    carrots,
She'll be eating French-fried
    carrots,
She'll be eating French-fried
    carrots when she comes."

"She'll be riding on a skateboard
    when she comes.
She'll be riding on a skateboard
    when she comes.

She'll be riding on a skateboard,
She'll be riding on a skateboard,
She'll be riding on a skateboard
  when she comes."

"She'll be smelling like a monkey
  when she comes.
She'll be smelling like a monkey
  when she comes.
She'll be smelling like a monkey,
She'll be smelling like a monkey,
She'll be smelling like a monkey
  when she comes."

The sillier the verses got, the more the boys laughed as they sang. When they got to their school, they ran to the back of the building instead of waiting at the front door with the other students. Tall grasses grew in the ragged field behind the building. In the distance, their gravel-covered track waited for runners, and the old wooden bleachers sat empty. Most of the athletic areas of their school were sadly in need of repair. They were not quite broken, but they were very old and cried out for modernization.

Ziggy and his friends paid no attention, however, to the grass-covered athletic areas, but stayed close to the building where there was more dusty ground than flowers. The shadow of the school building made it cool and shady where they stood.

"You ready to try our four-part harmony?" Rico asked.

"Yeah, mon!" Ziggy said excitedly. "Let's do it."

Jerome, who had a beautiful baritone voice, started out by giving them a note. Each boy then used it to find his own place in the four-part harmony. "Let's try 'Home on the Range,'" he said. "We'll start with the refrain. Ready?"

"Ready," the others said, paying close attention.

"Home," Jerome sang in a voice that was pretty close to baritone.

"Home," chimed in Rashawn's deep bass. Sometimes his voice cracked, but he was proud of how he could usually reach the low notes.

"Home." Rico's shaky tenor mixed in perfectly.

Finally Ziggy added his voice. "Home," he sang in a voice that was not quite tenor and not quite baritone, but always loud and enthusiastic. But he was on key, and the other boys nodded in approval as Ziggy hit the right note.

> "HOME, HOME ON THE RANGE,
> WHERE THE DEER AND THE ANTELOPE
>   PLAY,
> WHERE SELDOM IS HEARD,
> A DISCOURAGING WORD,
> AND THE SKIES ARE NOT CLOUDY ALL
>   DAY."

"Hey, now!" Jerome said with enthusiasm. "We sound really *good*!"

"Oh, yeah!" they all said in agreement, slapping hands.

"Should we sing that one for the tryouts?" Rico asked.

"We've got all day to decide," Rashawn said. "Let's get to class now."

Just then the bell rang and the four friends gathered up their book bags and scrambled to enter the building from the front. None of them noticed the car that was parked in the tall grass behind the athletic stands.

Two

The day seemed to trudge slowly as the four excited boys waited for the last bell. When it finally rang, they rushed down to the auditorium with the rest of the kids who were trying out for the talent show. Over a hundred boys and girls waited in the large, overheated room.

Mr. Cavendish, the music and drama teacher, was a chubby, cheerful man who was popular with all the kids. He stood on the stage and waited for everyone to get into a seat and quiet down. He didn't have to say a word; he just stood there silently.

"Cavendish is so cool, mon," Ziggy whispered to

Rico. "He makes sure that anybody who wants to be in the band has an instrument, whether they can afford it or not."

"Yeah, and he lets anybody be in the band, whether they can play it or not!" Rico whispered back. "He let you play the trombone last year, didn't he?"

"I gotta admit that was an experiment that bombed big time. I don't think the trombone was meant for me!" Ziggy laughed quietly.

"We were *all* glad when you figured that out!" Jerome, who was sitting on the other side of Ziggy, added. "My ears still hurt!"

Miss Blakely, the other music teacher in the school, sat on a wooden bench in front of the piano, ready to play for anyone who had not brought a background music CD. She was tall and thin with really skinny fingers, but she could play anything. Sometimes in class she'd play classical music, and sometimes she played what she called "boogie-woogie." Ziggy thought those songs were the best.

"May I have the attention of all the creative

young entertainers who are sitting in this room," Mr. Cavendish began. Every face in the audience was turned toward him. "Welcome to the tryouts for this year's talent show, which we're calling Stars and Sparks. I consider all of you to be talented beyond measure—full of what it takes to make you a success in life. In my book you are already stars, and you certainly have that magical spark of artistic expression."

"He must be talking about us," Rico whispered with a chuckle.

"Yeah, mon," Ziggy replied, his voice full of confidence.

Mr. Cavendish continued. "This talent show is designed not to choose a winner, but to allow you to showcase your skills, share your abilities with your families, and show the importance of the arts in our lives. Without music and drama and the arts, we are nothing. Are you with me, young entertainers?"

The audience cheered and applauded, even though some kids weren't sure exactly what Mr. Cavendish meant.

He took a breath. "What I mean to say is this show is not about winning. It's about sharing. I don't want to hear one word about who is better, or who is not so good. Do you understand?"

Ziggy jumped out of his seat and raised his hand. "Then why is there a two-hundred-dollar prize?" he asked.

Mr. Cavendish tried to explain. "The prize money was not my idea. Mr. Gordon from the Double-Good Grocery down the street wanted to help our struggling arts program, so they gave us a total of one thousand dollars—eight hundred to help students rent instruments, and two hundred as the grand prize for this contest. I appreciate the donation—really I do. But I don't want you kids to try out for this competition for the money. I want you to do it because you want to perform on stage, because you want to showcase your talents, because you want to be the best you can be."

Ziggy looked at Rico and Jerome and Rashawn. They nodded at each other. "Sounds good to me," Rashawn said.

"Let's begin then," Mr. Cavendish said. "I will call to the stage each group or individual who has signed up, and we'll all listen politely as everyone tries out. No one will make rude comments or noises. When each person has finished, the audience will applaud, and the next one on the list will try out. Everybody clear?" He waddled off the stage and stood in the front of the auditorium, a clipboard in his hand.

The first person called to the stage was Mimi, the shyest girl in their class. She trembled noticeably as she stood alone on the huge stage.

"She's terrified, mon," Ziggy whispered to Jerome.

Miss Blakely started to play the beginning of Mimi's song, but nothing came out of Mimi's mouth. She just stood there. Miss Blakely started the song again. Mimi started to cry. Mr. Cavendish headed back to the stage, but Ziggy beat him to it.

Ziggy sprang up from his seat, ran to the front and, ignoring the stage steps, leaped onto the stage from the floor. Mimi jumped a little in surprise.

"Not to worry, Mimi," Ziggy whispered in her ear. "Don't be scared. You know how silly I am. I'll be standing right here behind you, and if anybody in the audience says something, I'll make them eat my lunch! I've got one banana-pickle taco left over!"

Mimi looked at Ziggy with gratitude, smiled at his silliness, and relaxed. She looked over at Miss Blakely, nodded that she was ready, and the piano intro to "Michael, Row the Boat Ashore" began once more. Her sweet soprano voice rang out as clearly as the song of a bird on a summer morning. She never even noticed when Ziggy tiptoed from the stage and took his seat.

"MICHAEL, ROW THE BOAT ASHORE,
  HALLELUJAH.
MICHAEL, ROW THE BOAT ASHORE,
  HALLELUJAH.

SISTER, HELP TO TRIM THE SAILS,
  HALLELUJAH.
SISTER, HELP TO TRIM THE SAILS,
  HALLELUJAH.

RIVER JORDAN'S DEEP AND WIDE,
    HALLELUJAH.
MILK AND HONEY ON THE OTHER SIDE,
    HALLELUJAH.

RIVER JORDAN'S CHILLY AND COLD,
    HALLELUJAH.
CHILLS THE BODY, BUT WARMS THE
    SOUL, HALLELUJAH."

Everyone in the audience applauded thunderously when she finished, with Ziggy and the rest of the Black Dinosaurs hooting and cheering the loudest. Mimi looked around, a little amazed, and blushed as she ran to her seat. She whispered a small thanks to Ziggy as she hurried by the row where he sat. She did not stay in the auditorium but left with her mother, who had arrived to pick her up.

Mr. Cavendish, before he called the next name on the list, said to the crowd when they had quieted, "It's very difficult to be on stage alone, and it's especially hard to be the first one to try out. I'm proud of the support all of you showed Mimi." He paused and gave a nod of approval to Ziggy. "Our next group to try out calls themselves Snakes and Spiders. Would Bill and Tito come to the stage, please?"

Rico leaned over and whispered to Jerome and the others, "Remember when we had our backyard animal show? Bill owns that big old snake, and Tito has the pet tarantula!"

"Well, I hope they don't include the animals in their act," Jerome replied.

Bill and Tito's performance was a take-off on a heavy metal act, and they had even brought costumes for the tryouts. With two huge plastic snakes wrapped around their necks, cloaks around their shoulders that looked like spiderwebs, and black makeup on their lips, they looked pretty effective.

"I told you we should have worn costumes for the tryouts!" Ziggy said, bopping himself on the head.

"No, now they have nothing to surprise us with at the show. Our costumes will be a big surprise!" Rashawn reasoned.

"We haven't even decided what we'll wear, have we?" Jerome asked.

"Our costumes won't include snakes, will they?" Rico wanted to know.

"Of course not, mon," Ziggy answered. "We'll have to think of something really cool, though."

Bill and Tito had even brought their own background music. It was loud and metallic, about as different from Mimi's "Michael, Row the Boat Ashore" as ice cream is from hot sauce. It was very impressive, however, and everyone clapped with approval as they took their bows.

The next person to try out was Brandy, who read some of her original poetry to the delicate classical background music she had brought on a CD.

"She's pretty good," Rico said as she finished.

"I taught her everything she knows!" Ziggy said jokingly. Rico punched Ziggy on his arm.

Several more students sang songs, some in groups, some individually. A boy named Brian told jokes. He had everybody cracking up, even Mr. Cavendish and Miss Blakely. Another kid, Simon, astonished the audience by his skill at juggling—six rubber balls at one time. Several groups presented acts that included rap songs. Samantha, who sat next to Ziggy in math class, turned out to be an amazing magician.

Finally Mr. Cavendish called the Black Dinosaurs to the stage. "Let's do it!" Jerome said as the four boys ran to the front of the auditorium. "Old Smoky?" he asked, making sure they all agreed. Everybody nodded. They lined up on the stage, grinning with expectation.

"Uh, this isn't the song we're gonna sing at the show. Mr. Cavendish knows what it is, but we want it to be a surprise, so we're going to do our tryouts with this one called 'On Top of Old Smoky,'" Ziggy explained. "It's our own version—kinda silly—but it's full of sparks!" The four boys giggled a little, partly from nervousness, but also from the words they knew they were about to sing.

"We're also gonna have background music, but for today, Miss Blakely is going to play for us," Rico added. He nodded to the teacher, who started playing.

The four friends, trying hard to cover their smiles, began singing, their voices a little shaky, but on key.

"ON TOP OF OLD SMOKY
ALL COVERED WITH DIRT,
I LOST MY NEW BOOK BAG,
MY SOCKS, AND MY SHIRT.

I LOST MY UMBRELLA.
I LOST MY PET FROG.
MY FOOD IN MY LUNCH BOX
GOT ATE BY A DOG.

I LOST MY LEFT SNEAKER,
MY HAT AND MY COMB.
I LOST MY NEW TOOTHBRUSH.
I LOST MY WAY HOME."

All the kids in the audience began to laugh as the boys continued their song.

"ON TOP OF OLD SMOKY
ALL COVERED WITH ROCKS,
I LOST MY BEST BLUE JEANS,
MY COAT, AND MY SOCKS.

I LOST MY RED SNEAKERS,
AND MY UNDERPANTS,
AND ALL OF MY CANDY,
GOT EATEN BY ANTS.

IF YOU CLIMB A MOUNTAIN
ALL COVERED WITH DIRT,
HOLD ON TO YOUR BOOK BAG,
AND HANG ON TO YOUR SHIRT."

Everyone in the audience, including all the students, the parents who had come to pick up their children, and both the teachers were still laughing as they clapped and cheered enthusiastically for Ziggy and his friends as they took their bows and jumped off the stage.

"Use the steps, children," Mr. Cavendish reminded them, but by then the boys were already running up the aisle of the auditorium as everyone was still applauding. "All right, we still have a couple more people to try out. Let's settle down, folks," Mr. Cavendish warned.

"We rocked!" Rashawn whispered to the others as they sat down. The other three boys couldn't stop grinning. "We're in for sure, mon," Ziggy replied.

The last two groups to try out were dancers who jumped and twirled and spun across the stage to pounding drum music. One group did a jazz dance, while the other danced to African music. They were both fantastic, and once again the audience exploded in cheers of appreciation.

Finally, after everyone had had the opportunity to try out, Mr. Cavendish stood and spoke to the children. "Tomorrow," he said, "I'll post the list of participants in the talent show. I'm very proud of all of you. We're going to have a wonderful show this year. Thank you, and you are dismissed. If anyone does not have a ride home, let me know. I'll be by the

front door to make sure you're all out safely."

As everyone gathered up belongings and headed to the door, Ziggy glanced back. He grinned and waved good-bye to the stage, whispering, "We'll be back soon!"

Three

After the tryouts, Ziggy, Rico, Rashawn, and Jerome were just about the last to get ready to leave the school building. Since he knew the boys lived close enough to the school to walk home, Mr. Cavendish had asked them to stay and help him clear the auditorium and take materials back to his classroom.

"I love being in school when there's no one else here!" Ziggy said as he ran down the polished floors of the main hallway. His voice and the flapping of his tennis shoes echoed against the lockers and walls. "This is awesome, mon!"

"Yeah, school should be like this all the time," Rashawn said, agreeing with him. "Just the four of us all day long!" He jumped and leaped, trying to reach the ceiling.

"No teachers?" Rico asked.

"No girls?" Jerome mentioned, as he raced Ziggy down the hall.

"Just us, mon!" Ziggy said, laughing as he reached the far wall seconds before Jerome. "What do you think, Mr. C.?"

Mr. Cavendish had just come out of his class-room. "I think a school is just perfect when there are no students at all!" he said with a laugh. "Look how much work I could get done without kids in my room after school practicing a trombone!" He grinned at Ziggy.

"Ah, you know you love us, Mr. C.," Rashawn said. "Even when Ziggy was trying to learn the trombone!"

"You're right, fellas. You know where my heart is. But Ziggy and that trombone almost made me want to teach math instead of music!" All of them laughed.

"I think I'll try drums next," Ziggy said with a grin. "Lots of big noise!"

"Wait until I get earmuffs first!" Mr. Cavendish said, as he put his hands to his ears. Checking his watch, he said, "Thanks for your help, guys, but it's getting late. You better get on home now. Anybody want to use my phone to call your mom before you leave?"

Rico said, "Yeah, my mom knew we'd be late, but I'll call her and tell her we're on our way." He disappeared into the band room with the teacher. Jerome, Ziggy, and Rashawn sat on the floor outside the room and waited.

"A school smells different when it's empty," Rashawn said quietly.

"Yeah, like floor wax and stuff, mon," Ziggy said, agreeing.

"It feels like it's waiting," Jerome added, "for kids to show up and mess up stuff again."

Just then the silence was broken by a loud rattle and clatter, followed by a muffled scream. It seemed to come from a hall around the corner.

"What was that, mon?" Ziggy asked, jumping to his feet.

"I don't know. Maybe the custodian dropped something," Jerome replied.

"So why would he scream? Besides, that didn't sound like a man's voice," Rashawn added.

"Let's go check it out. Maybe somebody needs help, mon!" The three boys ran around the corner, only to find a stack of almost twenty chairs knocked over and strewn about the hall, and a girl about their age sitting in the middle of it all. She was holding her head in her hands.

"Are you okay?" Jerome asked as they ran over to the girl.

"I didn't mean to knock down the chairs," she said as she looked up. It looked as if she had been crying.

"Are you hurt?" Rashawn asked her gently. For once, Ziggy had nothing to say.

"One of the chairs bumped my head," she replied, rubbing her head carefully.

"Do you go to school here?" Rashawn asked. "I haven't seen you around."

The girl didn't answer. Even though the weather was quite warm, she was dressed in a dark blue woolen jumper, a dirty white long-sleeved turtleneck shirt, and boots—the kind a person would wear in the snow. The jumper looked old and well worn.

"I'm gonna go get Mr. C., mon," Ziggy said. He disappeared around the corner.

"What's your name?" Jerome asked the girl.

"Tulip," she replied with a small smile. "Like the flower." Her curly hair, most of which was hidden under a baseball cap, was almost the same color as her face—a dusty, tawny brown. Tulip seemed to be almost as thin as the stalk of a real tulip.

"That's a pretty name. Who's your homeroom teacher?"

Before she could answer, Mr. Cavendish, Ziggy, and Rico hurried around the corner. Tulip looked frightened and tried to stand up, but she promptly sat down again, holding her head. She started to cry once more.

Mr. Cavendish started to kneel down next to the girl; then, breathing hard, he gave up trying to kneel and simply sat on the floor. "Are you injured?" he asked, touching the girl gently on her arm.

Tulip felt her head, which was bleeding a little, and nodded yes. "Maybe just a teeny bit," she said, "but I'll be okay."

"Rico, go back to the phone in my classroom and call 911," Mr. Cavendish ordered. "Tell them we have an injured student here with a possible head injury. Hurry! Ziggy, go with him."

The girl looked alarmed. "You don't have to do that! Really, I'm fine."

Mr. Cavendish ignored her.

Rico looked thrilled to have the awesome responsibility of actually dialing those three important numbers. "He told *me* to dial, Ziggy! I'm the one who gets to talk to the cops!"

"Yeah, mon, but if you faint I'll be your backup!" The two boys hurried away.

Rashawn and Jerome looked jealous of Ziggy and Rico, but neither of them wanted to leave the injured mystery girl. The very large teacher and the very thin girl sitting in the middle of the almost deserted hallway made an unforgettable picture.

"I don't remember you at the tryouts," Mr. Cavendish said softly. "As a matter of fact, I know most of the students in this school, and I don't think I've seen you around here."

"I watched the tryouts," the girl said, wiping her eyes. "It was fun. I wish I could go to a cool school like this."

"What's your name, child?" Mr. Cavendish asked.

"Tulip Thompson."

"Where do you go to school?"

"Uh, I don't go to school. I mean, I used to go to school when my mom and I were in New Orleans, but . . ." She paused. "It's a long story."

"Where's your mother now?" Mr. Cavendish asked. "We need to call her right away."

"She doesn't have a phone," Tulip replied, looking down at the floor.

"Where do you live?" Mr. Cavendish asked then.

"Nowhere," the girl whispered. "I don't live anywhere at all." Jerome and Rashawn looked at each other, astonishment on their faces, but they said nothing.

The sirens could be heard in the distance then, and Ziggy and Rico, full of the responsibility and excitement of being the ones who had called the ambulance, ran back to where the others sat. "Go to the front door, then direct them to where we are," Mr. Cavendish said.

Ziggy and Rico darted off to the front of the school, racing to be first to the door. "This is so exciting, mon!" they heard Ziggy say as he ran.

Rico and Ziggy returned shortly with two uniformed members of the fire department—one man and one woman. They carried medical bags and equipment and walked with an air of authority. The woman knelt down next to Tulip, who looked a little overwhelmed at all the attention.

As the medics examined the girl and asked her questions, Ziggy and his friends stood close to Mr. Cavendish, watching the proceedings intently.

"Shouldn't you boys be going home now?" the teacher suggested.

"No way, mon!" Ziggy said. "Nothing this exciting has ever happened at school!"

"I called my mom back and told her we'd be late," Rico said. "She said she'd let Rashawn and Jerome and Ziggy's folks know, so we're cool."

"Do you think they'll take her to the hospital?" Jerome asked.

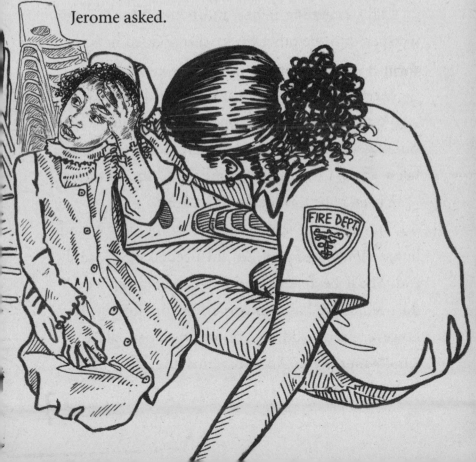

"I don't think she's hurt very badly—it's just a bump on the head," Mr. Cavendish said. "But I had to make sure. What concerns me is the location of her mother."

"Tulip! Tulip! Where's my daughter? Is she all right? Tulip?" A tired-looking woman ran into the building, her face full of alarm. "What happened? Why is the ambulance here?"

"This is getting better and better, mon," Ziggy whispered to the other boys, who nodded in agreement.

"Are you Mrs. Thompson?" the medic asked.

"Yes, I am. What happened? I left her for a few minutes while she watched the tryouts for the school talent show. I went to get some food," she admitted. "I've been gone less than half an hour."

"It seems she knocked over some chairs and bumped her head a bit. All she needed was a Band-Aid. She'll be fine, ma'am," the medic replied. "I do need some basic information for our records, however. Your address, phone number, place of employment, etc. And it seems the child is not enrolled in school—can you explain that, ma'am?"

Mrs. Thompson ran over to make sure Tulip was not hurt, gave her child a big hug, then took a breath. "We're from New Orleans. For several years it's just been me and Tulip," she began, as she combed her fingers through her daughter's tangled hair. "Our life was just fine. Tulip was in school, making good grades. I owned a little flower shop, which was in the front part of our house. We lived in back. Then Hurricane Katrina hit the city, and we lost everything. Our house was swept away."

Ziggy gasped. "Wow!" he whispered. "They were in a hurricane!"

"We've been moving around the country ever since, staying in various shelters and government housing while I tried to find work. When I got laid off my last job, we ran out of money pretty quickly, and we got evicted. We've been living in the car for a month or so. I know she needs to be in school, but I've just been overwhelmed." Mrs. Thompson hung her head.

For a moment everyone was silent. Then Jerome surprised himself by speaking up. "Come to my house for dinner. My grandmother *always* cooks too much food. I have two little sisters who would love to have a girl in the house, and my Granny would be angry if you don't come. I live just a block away."

"That's the nicest thing anyone has said to me in three weeks," Mrs. Thompson said, "but I couldn't impose on you like that."

"Mom, please?" Tulip said quietly. "I'm really hungry."

"Here's the address of a homeless shelter, ma'am," the medic said. They can give you a place to sleep tonight." He handed her a card.

"Thank you. We slept there the first night we arrived here," Mrs. Thompson said. "It wasn't the best place for my Tulip."

Jerome said, "I'm going to call Granny real quick and tell her you're coming." He darted down the hall and around the corner before Mrs. Thompson could protest.

When he left, Rashawn said, "Why don't you come to my house instead? I have a dog that Tulip can play with. His name is Afrika."

Then Rico joined in. "No, come to my house! It's just me and my mom there and you could join us in a meal of my mother's favorite boring food. I guess I shouldn't say that since I'm trying to convince you to come, but my mom can cook a meal from the four basic food groups, and everything on the plate will be beige!" He laughed at the thought. "Her cooking tastes good, though," he added with a grin.

Finally Ziggy said, "Forget all of them! Come to the home of Ziggy, where my mum will fix you Jamaican jerk chicken and her famous Jamaican pepper shrimp! And *all* the foods on our plates are a different color!"

"That's because Ziggy eats grape jelly on his tomatoes and puts green peas in his lemonade!" Rashawn said, teasing him.

Tulip looked confused and a little overwhelmed at all the attention the boys were paying her.

Jerome rushed back and told them, "Granny said '*please come*'!" She's already putting the plates on the table."

Mr. Cavendish told Tulip's mother, "I've eaten at

Jerome's house many times when his grandmother has picnics in her yard after our summer band concerts." He patted his very round stomach. "She's a wonderful woman and an even better cook. Her offer to come to her house is quite genuine."

Mrs. Thompson looked at Mr. Cavendish and the medics. "I apologize for any trouble we've caused. I promise to get Tulip enrolled in school right away— hopefully at this school. Thank you so much for all your kindnesses."

The medics left with instructions about caring for Tulip's bandage. Mr. Cavendish said finally, "Well, this has certainly been an unusual end to a very long Thursday." To the boys he said, "Gentlemen, I will see you tomorrow."

"Yeah, mon! You promised you'd have the list of who is in the talent show posted first thing Friday morning!" Ziggy reminded him.

"I remember." To Mrs. Thompson and Tulip he said, "I hope the next time we meet it will be under more pleasant circumstances." He made a tiny little bow to the two of them.

Tulip and her mother headed out to their car with Jerome, while the other three boys walked home, chattering with excitement. They had much to talk about.

Four

At school the next morning all the buzz was about the talent show tryouts and the mysterious new girl. Text messages and IMs and cell calls had spun like cotton candy among the kids at school all evening. Everybody had a different opinion about her, and nobody seemed to know the whole truth.

"I heard she's been hiding and sleeping in the basement of the school for a year—with fourteen cats."

"That's silly. Somebody told me she was from New Orleans and she almost drowned when Hurricane Katrina hit her house."

"No, I heard she ran away from a secret spy organization in Washington, D.C."

"For real? Then maybe that's why she was listening to our talent show tryouts."

"Somebody said they're homeless."

"I don't get it. Why can't her mom just get a job and find an apartment?"

"My uncle said people who are homeless just don't try hard enough."

"That's not nice. I feel sorry for them."

"Didn't somebody say she was Jerome's cousin from Kansas?"

"No, I think she might be one of Ziggy's relatives from Jamaica."

The three boys who knew the truth—Ziggy, Rico, and Rashawn—said nothing as the other kids gossiped and guessed about the new girl. Jerome had not yet arrived at school.

"Has Mr. Cavendish posted the results yet?" Brandy asked, finally changing the subject. "I hope he liked my poetry."

"I messed up," Mimi said sadly. "I don't think my name will be on the list."

Ziggy walked up to her then and said boldly, "Not to worry, Mimi. You sang real pretty yesterday. Really you did." Mimi blushed and smiled.

While waiting for Jerome, Rashawn and Rico sat with Ziggy in the front hall, which looked so different when it was filled with hundreds of kids and all the conversation and variety they brought. Noisy and bright, dressed in reds and greens and blues and khaki, the students made the hall come alive. It didn't seem like the same quiet place the boys had left the day before.

"Here comes Jerome." Ziggy didn't have to tell Rico and Rashawn. They, along with dozens of other kids, were staring at Jerome, who walked proudly next to Tulip up the front steps into the main hall. Instead of the torn jumper and the boots she'd had on the night before, Tulip wore a pale yellow flowered dress and matching sandals. Her hair, without the baseball cap, seemed to be a soft ball of glisten-

ing curls that bounced as she walked. The small
Band-Aid on her forehead could barely be seen.

"Wow, mon!" Ziggy said softly.

"Yeah. Wow," Rashawn and Rico
said at the same time.

Mrs. Thompson and Jerome's

grandmother followed them up the steps and headed for the main office, taking Tulip with them. Jerome joined the other three boys.

"Score two points for Granny," Jerome said as they slapped hands. "Probably more than that. Granny fell in love with Tulip and her mother. She made them both the biggest dinner we've had since Thanksgiving, then took them shopping to one of those stores that stays open all night, then tucked them both on the sofa for the night."

"Your granny is awesome, mon!" said Ziggy.

Rashawn commented carefully, "Tulip looks really, uh, different today."

"Amazing what a hot shower, a good breakfast, and a new dress can do for a person," Jerome said. "And this afternoon Granny is taking Tulip's mom to see about a job. Granny has a friend who owns a flower shop!"

"What would have happened if we hadn't met them?" Rico wondered.

"I'm glad she knocked those chairs down, mon," Ziggy said with feeling.

Tulip came out of the office with her mother just

as the bell rang for the first class. "Well, they called somebody in the office of the New Orleans school district and had my records faxed here, so it looks like I'm enrolled at your school," she said shyly as she looked at the class schedule in her hand.

Jerome asked her, "Can I see it?" He looked at it for a moment, then said with a smile on his face, "It looks like you have most of your classes with us!"

"I'll show you how to get to math class," Rico offered. "It's right down this hall."

"We're all going to the same place, mon," Ziggy said cheerfully. "Let the royal procession begin!" He headed down the hall as if he were marching in front of a line of soldiers. The other followed behind him.

"Is Ziggy always this silly?" Tulip asked.

"Nope. Most of the time he's sillier!" Rashawn replied.

In math class, the teacher, Mr. Landon, shook Tulip's hand and asked Ziggy and Jerome to introduce her.

"Uh, this is Tulip Thompson," Jerome said, feeling a little awkward. "We met her last night."

"She's lived a life of danger and adventure!" Ziggy added. "Fire engines! Ambulances! Medical emergencies! And lots of fried chicken from Jerome's grandmother." Tulip just waved to the class and took the seat that Mr. Landon assigned to her.

Mr. Landon, a short, muscular man with a face full of freckles, began his lesson on fractions. He asked Jerome to come the front to solve a problem on the board.

Jerome whispered to Ziggy as he got up, "I hate it when he makes us do this." He solved the problem without too much difficulty, but he was sweating when he sat down.

Mr. Landon then asked for a volunteer to do the next problem. Tulip raised her hand. Jerome turned around in surprise as Tulip made her way to the blackboard. Instead of being shy or embarrassed to do such a task on her first day, Tulip not only answered the problem correctly, but also showed two different ways to solve it. "I like math," she said quietly when the teacher congratulated her.

Their next class was English. In that class, Mrs. Powell took time to introduce Tulip to everyone and make sure she felt comfortable. Then she continued with the lesson from the day before, which was about poetry.

"We spoke yesterday," Mrs. Powell began, "about the power of words when we write them in poems, and how they can make us feel. I asked you to bring a favorite poem to recite to the class. Did anyone remember?"

Rico raised his hand. "I've got one!"

Ziggy said, "Me too! Me too!"

Mrs. Powell smiled. "Let's begin with your poem, Rico. Ziggy, we'll hear yours on Monday, okay?" Ziggy nodded in agreement.

Rico walked up to the front of the room, took a deep bow, and said, "This poem is called 'I Went to the Zoo with My Brother Magoo.'"

The kids in the class started to giggle.

"I WENT TO THE ZOO WITH MY

BROTHER MAGOO

AND A BOTTLE OF GLUE—AND

WHAT DID WE DO?

WE PUT EELS ON MY EYEBALLS, LIZARDS

ON MY LIPS,

SPIDERS ON MY STOMACH, AND HIPPOS

ON MY HIPS!

I WENT TO THE ZOO WITH MY BROTHER

MAGOO

AND A BOTTLE OF GLUE—AND WHAT

DID WE DO?

WE PUT BULLFROGS ON HIS BELLY,

TURTLES ON HIS TOES,

FALCONS ON HIS FOREHEAD, AND

RHINOS ON HIS NOSE.

I WENT TO THE ZOO WITH MY BROTHER

MAGOO

AND A BOTTLE OF GLUE—AND WHAT

DID WE DO?

WE PUT AARDVARKS ON MY ARMPITS,
   TIGERS ON MY TONGUE,
SEAGULLS ON MY SHOULDER, AND
   GORILLAS ON MY GUMS.

I WENT TO THE ZOO WITH MY BROTHER
   MAGOO
AND A BOTTLE OF GLUE—AND WHAT
   DID WE DO?

WE PUT ANTS ON HIS ANKLES, EAGLES
   ON HIS EYES,
FERRETS ON HIS FINGERS, AND TURKEYS
   ON HIS THIGHS.

I WENT TO THE ZOO WITH MY BROTHER
   MAGOO
AND A BOTTLE OF GLUE—AND WHAT
   DID WE DO?
GOT KICKED OUT OF THE ZOO!"

Rico took another bow and everybody in the

classroom cheered for him, but as Rico sat down, Ziggy jumped up and shouted, "I shoulda done that one, mon! That's a Ziggy kind of poem! Really awesome, Rico!"

Mrs. Powell seemed to agree as she made notes in her grade book. "Good job, Rico," the teacher said, still smiling, "And sit down, Ziggy!" He plopped back down in his seat. "Does anyone else have a poem to recite?"

Surprisingly, Tulip raised her hand. "Is it okay if I wrote the poem myself?" she asked.

"Of course, dear," Mrs. Powell replied. "Please come to the front. What is the title of your poem?"

"I call it 'The Blues for Kids.'" She stood without speaking for a moment, then began. She recited the poem from memory.

"I HEARD ABOUT THE BLUES, AND I
THINK THAT'S WHAT I'VE GOT,
BUT I'M NOT REALLY SURE WHAT THAT
MEANS.

I KNOW THAT I LIKE ALL THE COLORS
  BLUE CAN BE:
BLUE LIKE VELVET, BLUE LIKE OCEAN,
  BLUE LIKE JEANS.

IF WE DIDN'T HAVE THE BLUES, WE
  COULDN'T SEE THE STARS.
WE COULDN'T SEE A RAINBOW IN THE
  SKY.
NO GOLD OR RED OR PURPLE; NO
  ORANGE, PINK, OR GREEN;
JUST SHADOWS HUGGING RAINDROPS AS
  THEY SIGH.

I HEARD ABOUT THE BLUES, AND I
  THINK THAT'S WHAT I'VE GOT,
BUT I'M NOT REALLY SURE WHAT THAT
  MEANS.
I KNOW THAT I LIKE ALL THE COLORS
  BLUE CAN BE:
BLUE LIKE VELVET, BLUE LIKE OCEAN,
  BLUE LIKE JEANS.

Most of the kids in the class applauded enthusiastically. Brandy crossed her arms across her chest. Mrs. Powell looked stunned. "That was truly amazing, Tulip."

Tulip shrugged. "I like poetry."

"When did you write that?" the teacher asked.

"After the hurricane, when things looked really bad for me and my mom. I've been writing poems since I was five or six."

"Me too!" blurted Brandy, who looked a little upset that Tulip was getting so much attention.

"Brandy is also a very fine poet," Mrs. Powell told her. "You two should get to know each other."

Tulip smiled at Brandy, but Brandy reached down to dig in her book bag.

"We'll recite some more poetry Monday, class," Mrs. Powell said. Right now, let's turn to our grammar book. It's time to work on nouns and verbs." The class groaned as they reached for their books.

"Hey, mon!" Ziggy whispered to Jerome. "That Tulip girl is something else!"

Jerome grinned. "Yeah. I know."

Five

Mr. Cavendish's music class, which was choir instead of band this class period, was just before lunch. "Where's the list, mon?" Ziggy asked the teacher as he burst into the band room. "Who's going to be in the talent show?"

"Hold your horses, Ziggy," Mr. Cavendish said. He took attendance, introduced Tulip, who by now everybody already knew, and had everyone sing a few scales to settle the class down. "Now, class," the teacher said. "Let's work on our songs for the talent show. As you know, the audience will be expecting a wonderful show from not just the individual performances, but also from our choir. I'm very proud of the music awards you young people have won in the past couple of years. You are wonderful singers—all of you. Tulip, we welcome you to the choir."

"Do I have to try out for the choir?" she asked.

Mr. Cavendish chuckled. "No, we take anybody who signs up for the class—even Ziggy!"

"Hey, mon! I'm a dynamite singer! Want to hear a solo?" Ziggy stood and opened his mouth.

"No!" the whole class yelled as they burst into laughter.

Ziggy sat down then, laughing with them, and said, "You'll be sorry you missed this great opportunity before I go to New York and get famous!"

Mr. Cavendish announced then, "Let's try 'Mockingbird,' class. Are you ready?" Everyone nodded. "Remember now, even though our theme for the program is Stars and Sparks, this song is a lullaby, so let's sing it like we're trying to put a baby to sleep, okay?" He hit a note on the piano, and the room was filled with the pure, clear voices of the children in the class.

"HUSH, LITTLE BABY, DON'T SAY A
  WORD,
MAMA'S GOING TO BUY YOU A
  MOCKINGBIRD.
AND IF THAT MOCKINGBIRD DON'T SING,
MAMA'S GOING TO BUY YOU A DIAMOND
  RING.

AND IF THAT DIAMOND RING TURNS
  BRASS,
MAMA'S GOING TO BUY YOU A LOOKING
  GLASS.
AND IF THAT LOOKING GLASS GETS
  BROKE,
MAMA'S GOING TO BUY YOU A BILLY
  GOAT.

AND IF THAT BILLY GOAT WON'T PULL,
MAMA'S GOING TO BUY YOU A CART AND
  BULL.
AND IF THAT CART AND BULL TURNS
  OVER,

Mama's going to buy you a dog
named Rover.

And if that dog named Rover won't
bark,
Mama's going to buy you a horse
and cart.
And if that horse and cart falls
down,
You'll still be the sweetest little
baby in town."

"Lovely!" Mr. Cavendish said with pleasure, beaming at the class. "This is going to be the best program we've ever done! Now, we have one more person who wants to audition for the talent show," the teacher told the class then.

"Who's that? Everybody had their chance last night!" Ziggy said impatiently.

"Not everybody. Last night I met a young lady who whispered in my ear her desire to try out for our show, so if she's willing, I'm going to let her do that right now during class. Then I'll post the list this afternoon."

"Tulip?" Jerome asked.

"Tulip," Mr. Cavendish replied, nodding his head and motioning for the girl to come up to the front of the room. The rest of the class clapped for her in support.

Tulip walked slowly to the front, her eyes a little cast down, moving slowly and gracefully. She took a deep breath and began. When she began to sing, everybody in the room looked at each other in surprise.

Tulip belted out the song. Her voice was a deep alto, full and rich and strong. It was so loud and so dominating that Miss Blakely, who taught next door, peeped her head in the door just to listen.

"SWING LOW, SWEET CHARIOT,
COMING FOR TO CARRY ME HOME.
SWING LOW, SWEET CHARIOT,
COMING FOR TO CARRY ME HOME.
• • • •

I looked over Jordan, and what did
  I see,
Coming for to carry me home?
A band of angels coming after me,
Coming for to carry me home.

Swing low, sweet chariot,
Coming for to carry me home.
Swing low, sweet chariot,
Coming for to carry me home.

If you get there before I do,
Coming for to carry me home,
Tell all my friends I'm coming too,
Coming for to carry me home.

Swing low, sweet chariot,
Coming for to carry me home.
Swing low, sweet chariot,
Coming for to carry me home."

For a moment everyone in the classroom sat in stunned silence. Then, gradually, they began to clap, then cheer, then whistle and stomp with approval. Tulip smiled shyly and bowed again before she took her seat.

"Man," Rashawn said as he leaned over to whisper to Ziggy. "You'd think a little bitty thing like Tulip would have a teeny small voice like one of those talking dolls. But she's got a voice like one of those big church ladies whose voice sounds like it came from the bottom of a volcano. That girl can really blow it out!"

The boys looked at one another with concern. "She's good, really good," Ziggy whispered. The other three nodded.

"Where did you learn to sing that like, Tulip?" Mr. Cavendish asked.

Tulip shrugged. "I don't really know. We used to sing it in church back in New Orleans. I like music."

By the end of the day, everybody in the school either wanted to be Tulip's friend or was a little jealous of her because she seemed too perfect to be real.

She was the fastest runner during gym class when the teacher timed them on sprints.

"I like to run," she said when she finished, barely breathing hard.

In science class she knew the name of every single flower the teacher pointed to. "I like flowers," Tulip said with a smile.

Tulip suddenly became the most talked-about girl in the school. She was good at everything, but she was so sweet and shy that most kids ended up not resenting her at all. She also carried an air of mystery that made her the topic of many conversations.

"I'd hate to be homeless," Samantha whispered to Mimi as Tulip walked past them in the hall.

"Must be awful," Mimi replied. "No place to go to the bathroom or wash your hair."

"No television or microwave or video games or computer or telephone or CD player. No trips to the mall to get new clothes," Samantha said sadly.

"All you think about is stuff. With her mother out of work, they couldn't buy food. I hate being hungry," Mimi said.

"That would be terrible," Samantha replied. "No bed to sleep in. I heard they slept in her mom's car."

If Tulip overheard their conversation, she didn't let them know. She just quietly continued down the hall to her next class.

When the bell finally rang for the end of the school day, everyone who had tried out for the talent show ran to Mr. Cavendish's room to see the list of names of those who had been chosen to participate. Ziggy and his friends rushed to the front of the line. Tulip remained in the background.

Ziggy jumped with joy. "We're in, mon!" he cried with excitement. "The Black Dinosaurs are on their way to stardom!" Rico, Rashawn, and Jerome slapped hands with Ziggy, then they let other kids get close to the list to find their own names. Brandy was chosen to recite her poetry, and Mimi's name appeared on the list as well. She sank to the floor in relief. Brandy sat next to her and gave her a hug.

Several kids who had performed dance routines, three rap groups, a couple of rock groups, and Simon the juggler were on the list. Even Tito and

Bill, the Snakes and Spiders, had been chosen. The very last name on the list was Tulip.

"You made it, Tulip! You're going to be in the talent show!" Jerome told her.

"I'm glad," she said quietly. "I like talent shows."

Six

Saturday morning dawned bright and sunny,
and the Black Dinosaurs had decided to have an
early meeting. Ziggy got to the clubhouse first with
a broom he had borrowed from his mother. As
he swept the dust and leaves off the dirt floor, he
thought back to how he, Rico, Rashawn, and Jerome
had worked together to build this little shed in
Ziggy's backyard.

Using wood from an old fence, they had ham-
mered and nailed and struggled to get the walls to
stay up. The windows were simply holes cut into the
wood, and the door, which was closed with a piece

of bent wire hanger, didn't really lock anything in or out, but the clubhouse was theirs alone and therefore special.

Putting on the roof had been the hardest part, because the piece of fence they had used had been very heavy. Plus, it had been covered with little brown bugs that scrambled everywhere when they lifted it up, and Jerome hate insects of any kind. He had threatened to quit right then. With the help of lots of bug spray, they had been able to get the roof on, aided by two stepladders, a two-by-four balanced on a rock, and quite a bit of luck.

The clubhouse was about ten feet by twelve feet, which wasn't really big, but it was large enough for four boys to sit and talk. Their seating consisted of an old lawn chair, a folding chair that had been left over from a church picnic, a three-legged kitchen chair that used a big rock for the fourth leg, and an old bicycle with two flat tires. They also had a soft blanket to sit on that Ziggy's mom had given them.

Yeah, mon, Ziggy thought as he worked. *We sure could use that money to fix this place up.*

The four boys had held meetings here, done homework, goofed off, and even slept in the clubhouse overnight. In the winter Ziggy's father covered it with a big blue tarp, but little animals still managed to get in and try to make themselves at home.

Jerome arrived first, with a can of bug spray in his hand. "What's up, Ziggy? Need me to check for bugs?"

"You always do anyway, mon," Ziggy said with a grin. "Poor bugs don't have a chance with you around!"

Rashawn and Rico, who were racing each other through Ziggy's huge backyard, could be heard long before they got to the clubhouse.

"The raccoon path is always the fastest!" Rico shouted as he got to the door first. "Raccoons know what they're doing!"

"But I'm smarter than a raccoon!" cried Rashawn, touching the door seconds later. "That ought to count for something!" His dog Afrika, a Siberian husky with one blue eye and one brown eye, had, of course, beaten both boys running, and sat waiting for them.

"Smarter *maybe*, but not faster." Both boys laughed and grabbed a couple of the bottles of cold

water Ziggy's mother had provided for them.

"Passwords?" Jerome asked. When the boys had first started the club, they had decided to use a secret password to begin each meeting. The password meant nothing, really, but it added a sense of mystery to their club.

"Uh, let's see," Ziggy said, scratching his head. Ziggy never seemed to be able to remember the password. "I know! It's *mosquito*, mon! Jerome and his bug spray made me remember!"

The boys got comfortable in the clubhouse, munching on the brownies that Rico's mother had made for them. "Nothing better than chocolate," Rashawn said with his mouth full.

"Unless you add olives!" Ziggy said cheerfully.

"Ugh!" Rico said. The other boys watched with disgust as Ziggy plopped a dull green olive on top of each brownie before he gobbled it up.

"Yummy, mon!" Ziggy said, laughing at the looks on their faces. "You guys have no sense of adventure!"

They could hear birds singing from a tree in Ziggy's yard and the sound of a distant lawn mower as someone cut his grass. It was a perfect morning.

Rico finally asked what the others probably wanted to. "So, how's Tulip?" he asked Jerome casually, munching on another cookie. "How long are she and her mom gonna sleep on your sofa?"

"Granny left with them this early morning to look for a place for them to live," Jerome said. "Tulip's mom got the job at the flower shop, so I guess things are looking up for them."

"That's great news, mon," Ziggy said. "That girl sure can sing!"

"And run. And do math. And science. And English," Rashawn said.

"It is amazing how good she is at stuff," Jerome said, agreeing. "But she's so nice about it, most of the kids don't seem to mind."

"Do you think she'll beat us at the talent show?" Rico asked.

"No way, mon!" Ziggy said. "We've been practicing for weeks!"

"She's awfully good," Rashawn said, doubt in his voice. "What if she beats us?"

"You think she could?" Jerome asked. "That would be awful."

"Let's not focus on that. What can we do to make our performance better?" Rico asked, trying to sound positive.

"Let's add background music!" Rashawn suggested. "With drums!"

"Real music and drums have got to make our dance moves better," Jerome said with excitement. "Let's plan our costumes, too."

"How about doing something funny, mon?" Ziggy suggested. "Let's put some sparks in those stars!"

"Good idea!" Rico said. "Remember when we were little and we used to sing 'Fooba Wooba John'?"

"I don't think it will work for this show, but it sure was fun, mon," Ziggy said. They all started singing at the same time, each one acting out a verse. Ziggy stood up on a chair, pretending to kick at a tree.

"SAW A FLEA KICK A TREE,
FOOBA WOOBA, FOOBA WOOBA,

Saw a flea kick a tree,
Fooba Wooba John.
Saw a flea kick a tree,
In the middle of the sea.
Hey, John. Whoa, John,
Fooba Wooba John!"

The voices of the four boys, loud and silly, echoed in Ziggy's backyard. Rico jumped up next, pretending to be swimming.

"Saw a snail chase a whale,
Fooba Wooba, Fooba Wooba,
Saw a snail chase a whale,
Fooba Wooba John
Saw a snail chase a whale,
All around the water pail.
Hey, John. Whoa, John.
Fooba Wooba John!"

Rashawn, his long legs sticking out crazily, got down on the floor and pretended to jump like a frog. He knocked over the bicycle, and the others could barely sing for all the giggling.

> "SAW A FROG CHASE A DOG,
> FOOBA WOOBA, FOOBA WOOBA,
> SAW A FROG CHASE A DOG,
> FOOBA WOOBA JOHN.
> SAW A FROG CHASE A DOG,
> SITTING ON A HOLLOW LOG.
> HEY, JOHN. WHOA, JOHN.
> FOOBA WOOBA JOHN!"

Jerome, trying to be a cow and a cat and a dog, had all the boys of the floor, doubled up with laughter.

> "HEARD A COW SAY 'MEOW,'
> FOOBA WOOBA, FOOBA WOOBA,
> HEARD A COW SAY 'MEOW,'
> FOOBA WOOBA JOHN.
> HEARD A COW SAY 'MEOW,'
> THEN I HEARD IT SAY 'BOW WOW.'

Hey, John. Whoa, John.
Fooba Wooba John!"

The boys worked for the next couple of hours—
laughing, planning, singing, and dancing. They ate
all Rico's mom's brownies, then gobbled the cookies
that Ziggy's mom brought back to them a little while
later. They added a new section to their song, and
jazzed up the whole thing. When they finished they
were worn out, hot, and sweaty, but very proud of
themselves.

They were just about to call the meeting to a
close when a knock sounded on the door.

"More food?" Jerome said, holding his stomach.
"I'm stuffed!" He opened the door of the clubhouse,
expecting Ziggy's mom. Instead, standing there with
a smile on her face, was Tulip.

"Can I come in?" she asked.

Jerome was so flustered he shut the door in her
face.

Seven

"**It's Tulip!**" Jerome said, turning to his friends in confusion. "What should I do?"

"Why did you leave her standing there?" Rashawn asked.

"I didn't know what else to do!" Jerome kept wiping his hands on his T-shirt.

"You think maybe you should open the door?" Rico asked Jerome.

"We've never had a girl in here before," Jerome said nervously.

"So what? No girl has ever asked before, mon," Ziggy replied, trying to sound reasonable.

"It's a mess in here!" Jerome said, looking around at the candy wrappers, old soda cans, and pizza boxes that Ziggy had swept into a corner. Brownie crumbs decorated his dirty tennis shoes.

"It's always a mess—what difference does that make?" Rashawn said, chuckling a little at Jerome's distress.

"Are you just going to leave her standing out there, mon? Do something!" Sitting on the floor, Ziggy gobbled the last olive.

Tulip walked around to the side of the clubhouse, and stuck her head through the hole in the wall of the clubhouse that served as a window. "You know, I can hear everything you're saying," she said with a pleasant laugh.

Jerome looked even more embarrassed and said nothing. He sat down in one of the chairs, looking at his shoes.

"Come on in," Rico said. "The door isn't locked."

"I've only got a minute," she said, as she left the window and came around the corner. She opened their little door and walked into the clubhouse. It seemed suddenly smaller to the boys who sat there; they were a little overwhelmed.

"Well, this is it!" Rashawn said, his arms outstretched.

"We built it ourselves," Rico told her with pride.

"Awesome!" she said, looking around. "I like clubhouses."

"We're still working on it," Jerome said. "It's got a couple of rough spots. We're planning on doing lots of improvements after the talent show. If we win, that prize money will make this place off the hook."

"It's just perfect," she said with genuine admiration. "You guys are so lucky."

"You know, you're the first girl to ever set foot inside the clubhouse of the Black Dinosaurs!" Ziggy announced.

"That makes me feel really special," Tulip said with a smile. "Why do you call your club the Black Dinosaurs?"

"Well, when we first started the club, Rashawn had been interested in dinosaurs and archeology and stuff," Jerome explained.

"Yeah, he had this big old plastic dinosaur with him the day we started building, so we decided to name our club the Black Dinosaurs," Rico continued.

"That's it over there in the corner, hanging by that string," Rashawn said. He pointed to a dust-covered model of an apatosaurus.

"Cool!" Tulip said.

"So, what are you going to sing for the talent show?" Rico asked. "The same song you did for try-outs? You've got a great voice."

"Isn't it supposed to be a surprise?" Tulip replied with a grin. "What song are you guys doing?"

"She's right, mon!" Ziggy said. "Secrets rule!"

"I like the fact that Mr. Cavendish has made the theme of the show Stars and Sparks," Tulip said. "I haven't had much to laugh at lately, and this is going to be fun."

"It must be rough," Rico said, kicking at the dirt with his shoe, "not having a place to live and stuff." He stopped talking, not sure of what to say.

"It's no picnic," Tulip said. "Everything I ever owned got washed away in the flood waters. Our house was under ten feet of water. Everything was destroyed. My clothes. My stuffed animals. Things you don't think about like underwear and towels and toothbrushes. Plates and forks. My books. Pictures of me and my grandma. All gone."

"I don't know how I would have made it through all that," Rico said softly.

"You do, because you have no choice," Tulip replied. "But it was hard. They put you in a shelter with a hundred other people, and give you clothes that don't fit, and you feel like you'll never find your real self ever again."

"Deep." Rashawn sighed.

"We watched all the storm coverage on TV," Jerome said. "We even sent a collection from our school to the Red Cross."

"Lots of people tried to help," Tulip said, "but it was a rougher situation than anybody could imagine. So I'm glad to be in a place where I can laugh."

"It's great to be crazy sometime," Rico said, trying to lighten the feeling in the small cabin.

"Like that poem you recited in English class, mon," Ziggy reminded him, seemingly glad to change the subject. "But wait until you hear *my* poem on Monday! Nothing could be crazier!"

"Do you know the song, 'Boom Boom, Ain't It Great to Be Crazy'?" Jerome asked suddenly.

Tulip looked excited. "Yeah, I used to sing it at campouts with my friends at my old school."

"That ought to be my official theme song!" Ziggy said as he burst into song.

"BOOM, BOOM, AIN'T IT GREAT TO BE
    CRAZY?
BOOM, BOOM, AIN'T IT GREAT TO BE
    CRAZY?
SILLY AND FOOLISH ALL NIGHT LONG.
BOOM, BOOM, AIN'T IT GREAT TO BE
    CRAZY?"

Rico, Jerome, Rashawn, and Tulip joined in then.

"A HORSE AND A FLEA AND A COUPLE OF
    MICE
SAT ON A CORNER, EATING RICE.
THE HORSE HE SLIPPED AND FELL ON
    THE FLEA.

'Whoops,' said the flea, 'there's a
horse on me!'

Boom, boom, ain't it great to be
crazy?
Boom, boom, ain't it great to be
crazy?
Silly and foolish all night long.
Boom, boom, ain't it great to be
crazy?"

Tulip started the next verse, and the others followed.

"Way down South where bananas
grow
A monkey stepped on an elephant's
toe.
The elephant cried, with tears in
his eyes,
'Why don't you pick on somebody
your size?'

Boom, boom, ain't it great to be
  crazy?
Boom, boom, ain't it great to be
  crazy?
Silly and foolish all night long.
Boom, boom, ain't it great to be
  crazy?"

Ziggy gave them the words to the last verse, and they all sang the chorus as loudly as they could. With Tulip's strong voice, and the combined voices of the four boys, it was amazing how good they sounded, even singing that silly song.

"I called myself on the telephone
Just so I could hear that golden
  tone.
I asked myself out for a date,
So I said I'd be ready 'bout half-
  past eight!
• • • •

Boom, boom, ain't it great to be
  crazy?
Boom, boom, ain't it great to be
  crazy?
Silly and foolish all night long,
Boom, boom, ain't it great to be
  crazy?"

The five kids cracked up as they finished. The sound of a car horn could be heard honking not far away.

"That's my mom," Tulip said, a big grin on her face. "Wow, I haven't laughed like that in a long time. I just wanted to thank you guys for looking out for me. Especially you, Jerome, for offering us dinner and a place to stay. That was awfully nice of you."

Jerome looked flustered, but managed to say, "Uh, you're welcome. Granny likes to help folks."

"Well, she did lots more than that," Tulip said. "She helped my mom find a job, and this morning we found a place to live. It's not as nice as our old house, but it's a whole lot better than living in a car!" Her laughter was light and almost musical.

"That's great news," Rashawn said.

Tulip left then, waving good-bye, and headed back through the tall grass in Ziggy's yard to where her mother waited for her in the car.

"She's a nice girl," Ziggy said after Tulip left.

"Yeah, she is," Jerome said softly.

"She can still blow us away in the talent show, don't forget," Rashawn warned. "She's an awfully good singer."

"And she could use the money," Jerome added, sounding guilty.

Rico frowned. "But we've worked so hard to win this! I'm going back to my house now, and work on the CD of our background music," he told them. "There is no way the Black Dinosaurs are gonna get beat in this contest! Besides, we really need the money also. Look at this clubhouse."

"Yeah, mon!" Ziggy said, gazing at the broken chairs they sat on. "I'm going to get the drum music for you to add to the CD," Ziggy said.

"And my mom is going to help with our costumes," Rashawn said.

"And I'll keep working on our dance routine," Jerome added, getting back into the spirit of the competition. "We've got a lot to do. The talent show is Saturday!"

The rest of the boys agreed, and each one headed home to work on his part for the show.

Eight

Tickets for the talent show went on sale first thing Monday morning at school. Everyone who wasn't participating was eager to see those who were going to be in the show. Students lined up outside Mr. Cavendish's room to buy their tickets, some of them buying blocks of tickets for family and friends. A parent volunteer was helping with ticket sales, and lots of parents showed up to buy tickets as well.

Ziggy, Rico, Rashawn, and Jerome stood a little distance away, watching. "We're gonna have a big crowd for the show," Rico said.

"You scared about performing on stage?" Jerome asked.

"I'm not gonna be scared, mon!" Ziggy boasted. "I hope thousands of people show up!"

"It's different, you know, performing in front of real people instead of a room full of empty chairs," Rashawn reminded him.

"Yeah," Rico said. "We won't be able to see the people in the audience because the lights will be off. But we'll be able to hear them laugh or cough or clap."

"Hopefully there will be lots of clapping," Rashawn said.

"Well, we can be pretty sure Tulip will get lots of applause," Jerome said. "She might even win."

"She's good, but that doesn't mean she'll win the competition," Rico said reasonably.

"Mr. Cavendish said the show was more about performing than winning," Rashawn reminded them.

"Yeah, but the money sure would be nice, mon!" Ziggy said.

"We can spend our whole summer vacation fixing up the clubhouse," Rico said.

Jerome thought out loud. "Four brand-new chairs and a card table. A cooler to keep our soda in. Nice."

"I wonder how much a gallon of paint costs," Rico mused.

"What color should we paint it?" Rashawn said as the four boys headed to English, their first-period class.

"Purple on the outside and green and orange on the inside!" Ziggy said.

"No way, Ziggy!" Jerome said with a laugh.

"Okay, okay," Ziggy said, pretending to give in. "We'll make it orange and green on the outside and purple on the inside!" He ran ahead of the others so they couldn't punch him, but they chased him down the hall anyway.

"No running in the halls, boys," Mrs. Powell called as she watched them approach.

They slowed down, still giggling, and went to their seats.

"Make sure we don't put Ziggy in charge of buying the paint!" Rico said as he sat down.

"We're not gonna let Ziggy even *touch* the paint!" Rashawn said.

Tulip walked into the room just as the bell was ringing and she smiled at the four boys as she slipped quietly into her seat. She wore blue jeans and a pale blue T-shirt.

Mrs. Powell took attendance, passed back some papers from the week before, and took time to talk about the talent show.

"I'm really excited to see the show this weekend," she told the class.

"Wait till you see us perform," Ziggy said. "We're dynamite!"

"I'm sure all the performers will be wonderful," Mrs. Powell replied.

"Did you know first prize is two hundred dollars?" Rico asked.

"Yes, Mr. Cavendish told me. That's a lot of money," the teacher replied.

Bill boasted, "I'd buy video games!"

"Don't you first need a player to play them on?" Tito asked. "Your old one is broken, remember?"

"Video game consoles cost a lot of money," Brian said. "The good ones cost more than two hundred dollars."

"I'd buy cat food and two more cats," Tiana said. "I love animals."

"I don't want anything that eats or poops," said Max. "If I had two hundred dollars I'd buy a television with a DVD player in it. And a bunch of DVDs." He grinned at the thought.

"I'd buy clothes," Elizabeth said. "An outfit for every day of the week."

Mimi told her, "You'd run out of money before you ran out of days of the week."

"What would you buy, Tulip?" Jerome asked.

She thought for a moment. "I'd buy a big backpack and stuff to go in it," she said.

"Huh?" Jerome asked, scratching his head in confusion.

"Not a book bag, but a satchel with my special things in it to keep with me all the time. My own clothes and shoes. Stuff to fix my hair. Soap. Food—lots of food. My writing journal. A clean blanket." She paused. "And I wouldn't spend all the money; I'd keep a little bit extra in a safe place in the bottom of the bag." She looked away, seemingly embarrassed.

The class continued to chatter about the possibilities. Mrs. Powell interrupted them finally and said, "Maybe we should all write an essay for homework: What I Would Do with Two Hundred Dollars."

"Ah, man! Why is it that every time you have a conversation with a teacher, she turns it into a homework assignment?" Rashawn said to Jerome, groaning.

"Now you students know me well enough to know I had already planned to have you write that paper," Mrs. Powell said, ignoring Rashawn. "It's due on Friday. And it must include an advertisement that shows the cost of the items you'd purchase."

"But I'm not even in the talent show," said Max. "Why do I have to write the essay?"

"The essay is a homework assignment. It has nothing to do with the show. It's about dreaming and thinking of possibilities. Two hundred dollars isn't really as much money as you think. Things are very expensive these days." She looked thoughtful for a moment. "Yes, Max. You, and everyone in the class, has to write the paper. And I want you to find out how much the things you wish for will actually cost."

"What do you mean?" Mimi asked.

"Let me give you an example," Mrs. Powell replied. "Suppose I said I would use the money to buy myself some new shoes."

"Good idea," a boy from the back of the room called out. "Your shoes are pretty ugly!" The class giggled.

Mrs. Powell laughed. "Maybe so, but they're comfortable! Anyway, if I decided to buy new athletic running shoes, I might only be able to buy one pair with two hundred dollars. I'd have to find an advertisement that gave the price of those kind of shoes. But I might be able to buy three pairs of high heels if they were on sale at the department store. So I'd cut out an ad that showed the price of the high heels, and I'd include that with my paper."

"I get it!" Brandy said. "We have to write what we'd buy, and find something that tells how much that something would cost."

"Exactly!"

"Can we use the Internet?" Brandy asked.

"Of course! Just bring proof of the cost of the items you want to purchase. You're welcome to use the computer and printer here at school if you need to."

The class continued to complain, but the teacher was used to it and moved on. "Now, I think when we stopped our poetry study last week, Ziggy was the next to recite a poem. I've been thinking about this all weekend. Ziggy, you're on!" She sat down at her desk.

Ziggy swaggered to the front. "You all know," he began, "that I like to eat unusual stuff."

"Broccoli and potato chip sandwiches!" Rico called out.

"Chocolate-covered carrots!" Rashawn added, laughing.

"Peanut butter and pickles!" Jerome said.

"Well, it seems your friends know you quite well, Ziggy," the teacher said. "Even I have witnessed your famous food inventions. Now let's hear the poem."

Ziggy explained, "It's about going to the grocery store, sort of. It's just a silly poem, but it seems like it describes me. Here we go!" He took a big breath, grinned, and began. "'Popcorn and Pickles,' by Ziggy Colwin.

"Popcorn and pickles are my
    favorite treats,
hot sauce and syrup to drink!

So whenever I go to the grocery
    store
I climb in my cart just to think,
    and I think . . . and I think. . . .

Brownies and olives are my
    favorite treats,
mustard and chocolate to drink!

SO WHENEVER I GO TO THE GROCERY
  STORE
I CLIMB IN MY CART JUST TO THINK,
AND I THINK . . . AND I THINK. . . .

SPAGHETTI AND TOOTHPASTE ARE MY
  FAVORITE TREATS,
COFFEE AND KETCHUP TO DRINK!

SO WHENEVER I GO TO THE GROCERY
  STORE
I CLIMB IN MY CART JUST TO THINK,
AND I THINK . . . AND I THINK. . . .

CORNFLAKES AND GRAVY ARE MY
  FAVORITE TREATS,
YOGURT AND SOY SAUCE TO DRINK!

SO WHENEVER I GO TO THE GROCERY
  STORE
I CLIMB IN MY CART JUST TO THINK,
AND I THINK . . . AND I THINK. . . .

Liver and jelly are my favorite
  treats,
prune juice and mouthwash to
  drink!

So whenever I go to the grocery
  store
I climb in my cart just to think,
and I think . . . and I think. . . .
I think I'm gonna be sick!"

In between each verse, the class shouted "Ugh!," getting louder and laughing harder as the poem got sillier and the food choices got more disgusting. Ziggy took a bow and sat down, quite satisfied with himself.

Mrs. Powell, who was still wiping her eyes with laughter, stood up. "You wrote that, Ziggy?"

Ziggy nodded. "Really, I did. I was at the store with my mum, and I just started writing down silly food combinations. It was easy."

Mrs. Powell nodded in agreement. "That's how

the best poetry is created, class. Just like the poem that Tulip recited last Friday, poems come from things that are important to us."

"That's what I do," Brandy said. "I've been writing poetry since I was six years old!"

"Me, too," said Tulip quietly. The two girls looked at each other and smiled.

Mrs. Powell looked pleased. "Good for you, both of you. Save every single one of those poems. Each one is a moment of your life captured forever."

Nine

Ziggy, Jerome, Rashawn, and Rico rehearsed for the talent show every night after school. On Monday they practiced their dance moves with the new music Rico had created on his computer. The drums really made it come alive.

On Tuesday they figured out how to sing and dance at the same time—not an easy task. They'd get out of breath, and fall on the ground laughing, the music pounding on as they sat there trying to catch their breath.

By Wednesday, they'd worked out how to make the dancing and the singing work together. They'd sing a verse, then twirl, sing another verse, then stomp, then stop singing altogether, and the four of them would leap and twist to the music.

Thursday they practiced with their costumes on. All of their parents had pitched in. Rico's mother made the outfits—shiny black slacks and satin shirts to match. Rashawn's mother made four capes with colorful satin linings that swirled when they moved. Jerome's cape was bright blue, Rico's bright green, Rashawn's a deep purple, and Ziggy's a blazing orange.

Jerome's grandmother had gone to the local costume store and found four shiny

plastic top hats to match the capes—one orange, one blue, one green, and one purple. Ziggy's mom sewed sparkles on everything.

"Awesome!" Ziggy whispered as they modeled the outfits.

By Friday, they were ready. The four boys went to school that morning, swaggering a little with confidence.

"Just wait until tomorrow!" Rashawn told everyone boldly.

"I already got my tickets!" one boy said in response. "I can't wait to hear what you guys come up with."

"The Black Dinosaurs will rule the talent show!" Jerome said, echoing him. "Just call us the Lyrical Miracles!"

"Better than the Dance Machine?" Tito asked. "My sister's in that group."

"I'm sure your sister is really good, mon," Ziggy told Tito. "But our dance moves are so outstanding they want to use them in a music video!"

Tito had to laugh. "You're so full of stuff, Ziggy."

"Our costumes will blow you away!" Rico boasted. "They were flown in from Europe last night!"

"For real?" Mimi asked.

Brandy told her, "Don't believe anything they say. Their moms made the costumes."

"I knew that," Mimi replied. But she looked a little embarrassed.

"Be there if you dare!" Jerome said.

Just then, Tulip came up the steps and into the front hall. She wore the same blue jeans and T-shirt almost every day.

"Hey, Tulip," Jerome said. "Are you ready for the talent show? Do you have your costume?" Rico, Rashawn, and Ziggy hovered close by.

She smiled shyly. "I haven't had much time to practice, and I don't have a costume, but I'll do my best. I'm just glad I get to be in the show."

After all the loud and silly boasting of the Black Dinosaurs, Jerome didn't know what to say to Tulip. He looked down at the floor.

"Did you and your mom get settled in the new place?" Rico asked her.

She sighed. "Yes, it's tiny, and the furniture in it is kinda old and beat-up, but it's home! Momma is really happy. She hates having to depend on other folks for stuff. She'll be baking cakes and making bouquets for Jerome's grandmother for the next five years so she can thank her!"

"Sounds good to me!" Jerome said, looking up and smiling once more.

He walked with Tulip to English class, where the chatter was about the talent show and Mrs. Powell's homework assignment.

"Does anybody have an extra ad I can use?" Brian asked. "I couldn't find anything that advertised monkeys."

"Who'd want to buy a monkey anyway?" Liza asked, making a face. "That's a dumb use of two hundred dollars!"

"I want to start my own zoo," Brian explained.

"You're going to need millions of dollars for something like that," Rashawn said.

"And remember the mess that happened at my house when we got all those animals together, mon?" Ziggy said. "Running a zoo is a *lot* harder than you think!"

Everyone who had been there that day laughed, remembering the chaos and confusion.

Mrs. Powell began class, saying, "I know everyone is excited about the talent show tomorrow, so let's have an easy day today. We'll let one person read his or her essay to the class, then we'll finish early, because I brought doughnuts as a treat!"

Everyone in the class cheered.

"Did you remember onions to go with mine?" Ziggy asked, laughing.

The teacher made a face. "Sorry, Ziggy, I just couldn't bring myself to do that."

"Not to worry. I always carry my own!" Ziggy pulled an onion from his book bag.

When she got the class settled again, Mrs. Powell asked for a volunteer to read his paper. Simon, a tall, quiet boy with straight blond hair, went first.

"If I had two hundred dollars, I'd buy books. I used to hate reading. In second grade, we'd sit in a big circle and everybody would read a paragraph out loud. It was awful. I always felt stupid. When I didn't know a word, the smart kids would giggle and I'd start to sweat. The teacher would try to give me a hint, but I'd be so confused that I couldn't even remember what the sentence was. The teacher would finally sigh, then tell me the word. I'd say it real fast and try to go on, praying that there wouldn't be any more hard words hiding on the next line, and praying for a fire drill or a tornado."

Simon stopped for a moment and looked up from his paper. Lots of kids seemed to be nodding in agreement. He continued:

"By the time my turn was finally over, my brain would be blank. The teacher would ask stupid questions like, 'Why was Silly Sam so happy?' I'd never even have a clue. Silly Sam was probably happy because he didn't have to read out loud at school.

"I probably never would have got out of second grade and I'd probably still hate reading if it hadn't been for that student teacher we had. His name was Mr. Stanker and he looked really young for a teacher. We giggled when we heard his name. Of course we called him Stinker Stanker. He had pimples on his face, and his hair was cut in a buzz, and he dressed like a teenager, but he made reading fun. He made up games for us to guess words, let us play Scrabble instead of making us take spelling tests, and lots of times he read to **us**! He had a deep voice that made the stories seem real and exciting.

"Sometimes he'd use words that were

bigger than my whole head. But he'd stop and explain if he thought we didn't understand. When it was our turn to read, he would give us a private time to do it. That way I didn't make so many mistakes, and I remembered the stories and ideas. I think I learned to like books that year. So, because of a teacher named Stinker Stanker, I'd buy two hundred dollars worth of books. The end."

Simon sat down, looking a little embarrassed.

"That was excellent, Simon," Mrs. Powell said.

"Oh, here's my advertisement for books. It came in the Sunday paper," Simon added. "Can we have our doughnuts now?"

"Speaking of books," Mrs. Powell said, "I've got a poem to share with all of us. Actually, it's a rap." She grinned. "We can learn it while we eat our snacks."

"No way, mon!" Ziggy said. "Teachers don't

know how to rap." He and the other kids nodded in agreement.

"It's called 'Reader's Rap,'" Mrs. Powell said after she passed out the treats. "Just repeat the chorus after me. Left side of the room first. Then the right side. Ready?"

Everyone in the class looked dubious, but curious. Mrs. Powell inserted a CD into the player and a clever hip-hop rhythm filled the room.

"Say hey hey! I read a book today!" Mrs. Powell began. She pointed to the kids on the left side of the room.

"Say hey hey! I read a book today!" they repeated.

"Say yo yo! I'm gonna read some mo'!" She pointed this time to the right side of the room, making her voice sound low.

"Say yo yo! I'm gonna read some mo'!" the students responded loudly and enthusiastically.

"In a book I find the magic.
In a book I find the key.

When I read my brain is busy.
When I read my mind is free!"

Mrs. Powell read with a flair, then pointed to the students on the left once more. They were ready and excited as they repeated the chorus.

"Say hey hey! I read a book today!"

"Say hey hey! I read a book today!" Simon, in the group on the left, smiled with pleasure as he chanted with the others.

"Say yo yo! I'm gonna read some mo'!" Mrs. Powell said to the kids on the right.

"Say yo yo! I'm gonna read some mo'!" Ziggy was out of his seat, dancing to the rhythm of the poem.

"In a book I find the answers.
In a book I find the clues.
When I read I am the captain.
When I read I NEVER LOSE!"

Mrs. Powell was enjoying herself. "Say hey hey! I read a book today!"

"Say hey hey! I read a book today!" the left side said loudly.

"Say yo yo! I'm gonna read some mo'!"

"Say yo yo! I'm gonna read some mo'!" the right side yelled even louder.

"With a book I have the victory.

With a book I have a friend.

With a book I am a champion.

With a book I always win!"

"Say hey hey! I read a book today!"

"Say hey hey! I read a book today!"

"Say yo yo! I'm gonna read some mo'!"

"Say yo yo! I'm gonna read some mo'!"

By this time the whole class was out of their seats and chanting to the rhythm of the rap. They cheered when it was finished.

"That was hot, man," Rashawn said.

"I told you," the teacher said cheerfully and triumphantly. "Let's clean up, then we'll go down to the auditorium and help Mr. Cavendish finish the decorations for tomorrow."

"She is one cool teacher, mon!" Ziggy said as he munched his doughnuts and onion.

Everyone had to agree.

Ten

The weather on Saturday was balmy and pleasant. Rain was predicted for Sunday, but this evening was turning out to be perfect. Hundreds of tickets had been sold, and excitement was at a fever pitch. It was not quite dark yet, but the parking lot outside the school was already filling up. Dozens of parents, some carrying bouquets of flowers to give to their kids after the show, most carrying cameras, filed through the ancient auditorium doors to sit in the wooden seats.

Tiana and Liza, who weren't in the show, had been chosen, along with several other kids, to be ushers. Dressed in black skirts and white blouses, they passed out programs and made sure people could find a seat.

The band began warming up, and parents waved and took pictures of their children who were playing instruments.

Backstage, some of the participants chattered nervously, while others sat quietly, going over their lines. Two boys scuffled over a piece of gum. One girl threw up. Tensions ran high.

"I can't find my shoes!" Brandy yelled. "Who stole my red shoes? I can't perform without those— they're my lucky shoes!" She looked frantically in everyone's bag, and even behind the scenery.

"You're wearing them," Mimi told her quietly.

Brandy looked down, sighed with relief, and sat down in a heap on the floor. "I'm losing it!" she said as she put her head in her hands.

"Is the choir ready?" Mr. Cavendish asked. "You're on first, to set the tone for the individual and group performers."

The choir members, dressed in the school colors

of blue and yellow, nodded nervously. Most of the boys wore blue; most of the girls wore yellow. Tulip, in the yellow dress she'd worn on her first day at the school, fit in perfectly.

Ziggy, Rashawn, Jerome, and Rico, dressed in blue slacks and yellow shirts, had their costumes for their performance backstage waiting for them to change into.

"Let's get this show on the road, mon!" Ziggy said nervously.

The choir lined up on the risers, and the curtains opened with a swoosh. The children, illuminated by the stage lights, inhaled with excitement as the audience erupted into thunderous applause.

"I can't see anything past the first row," Jerome whispered to Rashawn who stood next to him. "Except for a few flashes of people's cameras."

"Me, neither. It's like a huge blob of noise and thunder out there."

Mr. Cavendish bowed, and the audience quieted and waited with anticipation. "Welcome to our talent show!" he said with pride. "Your children have worked very hard to make this production a success. And yes, although there is a cash prize being offered tonight, I've tried to stress to them that we are doing this simply for the joy of performing. Let's hear it for music for its own sake!"

The parents seemed to like this idea, for they applauded enthusiastically once more.

"Since it's near the end of the school year, we decided to try to have some fun tonight. Our theme is Stars and Sparks. We'll begin with a song that includes both. Please rise for our national anthem."

He turned his back to the audience and faced the choir. He nodded to Miss Blakely, who was directing the band, and the first strains of "The Star-Spangled Banner" could be heard puffing from the sixth-grade students on tubas and trombones and trumpets.

On the signal of Mr. Cavendish, the choir members sang clearly,

"OH, SAY CAN YOU SEE,
BY THE DAWN'S EARLY LIGHT,

WHAT SO PROUDLY WE HAILED
AT THE TWILIGHT'S LAST GLEAMING?

WHOSE BROAD STRIPES AND BRIGHT
  STARS,
THROUGH THE PERILOUS FIGHT,
O'ER THE RAMPARTS WE WATCHED,
WERE SO GALLANTLY STREAMING?

AND THE ROCKETS' RED GLARE,
THE BOMBS BURSTING IN AIR,
GAVE PROOF THROUGH THE NIGHT
THAT OUR FLAG WAS STILL THERE.

O SAY, DOES THAT STAR-SPANGLED
BANNER YET WAVE
O'ER THE LAND OF THE FREE
AND THE HOME OF THE BRAVE?"

Mr. Cavendish and choir bowed, and the audience, already in a good mood, clapped and waited for the next song as they sat back down. The choir sang all ten verses of "Billy Boy" and then did a beautiful version of "Mockingbird."

"Now, ladies and gentlemen, let's begin the competition part of our program. Our first contestant is a young lady named Brandy, who writes her own poetry. Let's give her a big round of applause!"

The curtain slid shut, and Brandy, dressed in a new red dress, walked out onto the stage in front of the closed curtain. Her lucky red shoes clicked on the hardwood floor.

"Hi, my name is Brandy, and I like to write poetry," she began. She motioned to a girl sitting with the band who was operating a CD player, and her background music began. It sounded rich and jazzy, something you might want to dance to. "The name of my poem is 'The Colors of We.'

"BROWN IS WARM AND BROWN IS GOOD.
BROWN IS EARTH AND BROWN IS MUD.

I AM WARM AND I AM GOOD.
I LOVE EARTH AND I LOVE MUD.

Black is cool and black is bright.
Black is dreams and black is night.

I am cool and I am bright.
I love dreams and I love night.

Green, green, my arms are green.
What shall I do? What does this
  mean?

Blue, blue, my nose is blue.
What shall I do to look just like
  you?

Red, red, my legs are red.
I know what they think; I heard
  what they said.

I think I'll keep my arms so green
I'll get a gold crown and I'll be a
  queen.

. . . .

I think I'll keep my nose so blue
I like being me and not being you.

I think I'll keep my legs so red
I'm not like all the others—I'll be
myself instead!

Brown is black is red is blue
Green is gold is me is you!"

Her music stopped, she took a bow, and the audience clapped loudly for her. She walked off the stage, red shoes clicking, and before she reached the edge of the curtain, she said loudly, "Whew! I'm glad that's over!" The people in the audience giggled a little as she disappeared behind the big blue drape.

The next performers, the combo called Dance Machine in which Tito's sister performed, were dancers whose act was a combination dance team/cheerleader/gymnastics routine. The music was loud and funky, and the five girls in the group jumped and twisted and leaped all over the stage. When they finished, breathing hard and sweating heavily, even the people in the audience seemed to be exhausted. The group got a round of rousing applause, however.

Mimi's quiet but powerful singing was next. Even without Ziggy's help this time, she performed beautifully. Her mother came up to the front, squatted down low, and took pictures throughout Mimi's presentation. Her mother clapped louder than anyone when she took her bow.

Even though Simon dropped a couple of rubber balls, he managed to complete his juggling routine. Samantha's rabbit refused to come out of the hat, but the rest of her illusions were just plain magical. Several more singers and dancers performed, all of them enthusiastic and energetic. Bill and Tito's act was a big hit. Finally only two acts remained—Tulip and the Black Dinosaurs.

Tulip took the stage in her pale yellow dress and sang in a voice big enough to fill the auditorium, even without a microphone. She used no backup CD or band music.

"HE'S GOT THE WHOLE WORLD IN HIS
HANDS,
HE'S GOT THE WHOLE WORLD IN HIS
HANDS,
HE'S GOT THE WHOLE WORLD IN HIS
HANDS,
HE'S GOT THE WHOLE WORLD IN HIS
HANDS."

As she began the next verse, Tulip took her voice down very small. It was softer, but just as powerful.

"HE'S GOT THE LITTLE BITTY BABY IN
HIS HANDS,
HE'S GOT THE LITTLE BITTY BABY IN
HIS HANDS,
HE'S GOT THE LITTLE BITTY BABY IN
HIS HANDS,
HE'S GOT THE WHOLE WORLD IN HIS
HANDS."

. . . .

It seemed as if she ended the song with even more power than she had started with. She held her arms out like a Broadway star concluding a show, with her head tilted back and her eyes closed.

"He's got you and me brother, in
His hands,
He's got you and me sister, in His
hands,
He's got you and me brother, in His
hands,
He's got the whole world in His
hands!"

When she finished she took a low bow. The audience was stunned. Then they stood and clapped and cheered. No one else had received a standing ovation.

"We got our work cut out for us," Jerome said, peeping from behind the curtain. "She was terrific!"

"Not to worry, mon!" Ziggy said as they listened to the applause. "We've got the best performance. Right?" He looked a little worried.

The four boys waited nervously for their turn. With their colorful, shiny top hats, matching sparkle-covered capes, and black satin shirts and slacks, the four boys looked truly professional. Their colorful accents—Jerome's blue, Rico's green, Rashawn's purple, and Ziggy's orange—glimmered in the dim backstage lights.

"We look like rock stars!" Rico said as they looked at one another in the backstage mirror.

Ziggy twirled with the cape and bowed with the top hat to Mimi and the other kids backstage who admired the four boys as they got ready. "I'm gonna wear this to school every day, mon! I look *too* good!"

"It's time, boys," Mr. Cavendish said. "You're our finale—make it wonderful!"

The stage, completely dark and completely silent now, suddenly erupted in Jamaican drum rhythms. Then green, purple, blue, and orange spotlights decorated the stage. Into those lights stepped Rico, Jerome, Rashawn, and Ziggy. All was drums and lights and drama.

"Day-o, Day-o," they began. Rico's music kicked in then, a wonderful mix between calypso and hip hop.

> "DAYLIGHT COME AND ME WANNA GO
>   HOME.
> DAY-O, DAY-O."

They paused dramatically.

> "DAYLIGHT COME AND ME WANNA GO
>   HOME."

The four boys began to dance. Their well-rehearsed steps perfectly matched the rhythms and the drums and the music. Their colorful capes swirled. The audience began to move and clap to the music.

> "COME MR. SILLY MAN, PEEL ME A
>   BANANA.
> DAYLIGHT COME AND ME WANNA GO
>   HOME.

COME MR. SILLY MAN, PEEL ME A
BANANA.
DAYLIGHT COME AND ME WANNA GO
HOME.

DAY-O, DAY-O,
DAYLIGHT COME AND ME WANNA GO
HOME.
DAY-O, DAY-O,
DAYLIGHT COME AND ME WANNA GO
HOME.

A BEAUTIFUL BUNCH OF RIPE BANANA!
DAYLIGHT COME AND ME WANNA GO
HOME.
HIDE THE DEADLY BLACK TARANTULA!
DAYLIGHT COME AND ME WANNA GO
HOME.

EAT SIX FOOT, SEVEN FOOT, EIGHT FOOT
BUNCH!

DAYLIGHT COME AND ME WANNA GO
HOME.
I EAT TEN BANANAS FOR MY LUNCH!
DAYLIGHT COME AND ME WANNA GO
HOME.

DAY-O, DAY-O,
DAYLIGHT COME AND ME WANNA GO
HOME.
DAY-O, DAY-O,
DAYLIGHT COME AND ME WANNA GO
HOME. . . ."

They paused, but the drums kept vibrating. They removed their hats, and slipped smoothly into the second song, ending and beginning on the same word: *home.* The music switched a beat and slowed down just a little. They sang, in perfect four-part harmony,

"HOME, HOME ON THE RANGE,
WHERE THE DEER AND THE ANTELOPE
PLAY,

Where seldom is heard a
discouraging word,
And the skies are not cloudy all
day.

Oh, give me a home where the
buffalo roam,
Where the deer and the antelope
play,
Where seldom is heard a
discouraging word,
And the skies are not cloudy all
day."

As they sang the word *day*, the beat of the music sped up, the boys put their top hats back on, and *day* became the first word of "The Banana Boat Song." It was a slick transition.

"Day-o, Day-o,
Daylight come and me wanna go
home.

Day-o, Day-o,
Daylight come and me wanna go
home.

Come Mr. Silly Man, peel me a
banana.
Daylight come and me wanna go
home.
Come Mr. Silly Man, peel me a
banana.
Daylight come and me wanna go
home."

The four boys ended their performance as they began—dark stage, four brightly colored spotlights, heads bowed. The music became softer and finally stopped.

Shrieks, whistles, and stomps erupted from the crowd. "Bravo! Bravo! Hey, now! Awesome!" the people in the audience chanted. Rico's mom shouted over all the noise, "That's my boy up there! That's my baby boy!"

The four boys kept taking bows, and the audience kept cheering. Ziggy motioned to the rest of the kids who were standing offstage, and all of the other participants, along with Mr. Cavendish, crowded onto the stage to take their final bows. Brandy in her red dress and shoes, the magician, the dancers, the rappers, the singers—all of them stood grinning with pride at the explosive applause and appreciation that was coming from the audience.

"See what I mean?" Mr. Cavendish told the kids on the stage as they gave him hugs around his large waist. "This is what it's all about! There's nothing better than the roar of the crowd as they thank you for entertaining them well."

"Do you think we nailed it?" Rico whispered to Ziggy as all the performers took more bows.

"I think Tulip blew us away, mon," Ziggy whispered back.

"She was dynamite!" Rashawn added, joining hands with the others as the whole cast bowed as one.

"Maybe we don't deserve to win," Jerome reasoned, joining in the whispers, although no one could hear them over all the cheering and stomping with the satisfaction of a show well done.

"We worked so hard on this. I think I'd feel bad if we lost," Rashawn said, frowning a little in spite of the joy all around him.

"I think I'd feel bad if we won, wouldn't you?" Ziggy asked, but his question went unanswered because Mr. Gordon, the owner of the Double-Good Grocery, walked onto the stage as the audience quieted.

The performers waited on the stage, huddled together. Tulip stood very close to Jerome.

"I have truly enjoyed watching the students perform here tonight," the tall gentleman in the business suit announced to the crowd. "We believe in supporting our schools, and we will be making a sizable donation to the music department here to make sure this kind of program continues."

The crowd cheered and clapped again. The

grocery representative held his hand up to get everyone's attention once more. "And although we feel that everyone who performed here tonight was a winner, the first-prize winner of the two hundred dollars goes to . . ." He paused for effect and looked at all the children on stage. ". . . the group called the Black Dinosaurs!"

Everyone on the stage roared with approval as they all hugged the four boys in congratulations. The audience's cheers and applause showed their approval as well. Ziggy, Rashawn, Rico, and Jerome made their way to the front of the stage, looking a little dazed as the man gave them an oversized check made out for two hundred dollars. Ziggy took it and held it aloft, grinning triumphantly. Mr. Cavendish stood next to them, beaming with delight.

"Which of you wishes to speak for the group and thank Mr. Gordon?" Mr. Cavendish asked.

Ziggy raised his hand. "Uh, I'll talk, but can I have one second to talk to the rest of my group, sir?" Mr. Cavendish and Mr. Gordon nodded, and the people in the audience quieted, waiting to see what was happening. Ziggy and the rest of the Black Dinosaurs huddled together for less than a minute, their capes draped across

their shoulders, making them look a little like a multicolored bird on the stage.

"You think we ought to?" someone heard Rico whisper.

"Yeah, mon!"

"We're agreed, right?"

"Cool!" The four boys broke out of their huddle and walked together to the microphone. They were smiling widely.

Ziggy took the microphone in his hand and took a deep breath. Rashawn, Jerome, and Rico stood next to him. Ziggy turned toward Mr. Gordon and grinned. "This is way cool, mon!" Mr. Gordon smiled broadly and the people in the audience chuckled. "And we really want to thank you, sir, for the money." The audience clapped politely.

Ziggy spoke a little louder. "We planned to use the cash to fix up our clubhouse new table and chairs, maybe a little orange and purple paint." He grinned as Rashawn punched his arm. "Our clubhouse is a place we play in; it's just for fun. But we met a family in the past few weeks that could use the money to help fix up a real house, so we've decided to donate it to them instead."

Again, the audience exploded in applause.

"What a wonderful group of young people you are!" Mr. Gordon said with approval. "I'll tell you what—we'll double your gift to them, and offer them free groceries for a month! How does that sound?" Everyone in the room cheered.

Ziggy and his friends the Black Dinosaurs all shook hands with Mr. Gordon then. Rico's mother ran up on stage to take pictures.

Mr. Cavendish dismissed the audience then, and real chaos took over. Parents rushed on stage to hug their children, offer them flowers, and take hundreds of pictures. Everyone, it seemed, wanted to hug or shake hands with the Black Dinosaurs.

When the crowd had thinned, and all the costumes had been collected and lost hair ribbons and sweaters had been placed in a pile, Ziggy and his friends waved good-bye to Mr. Cavendish, who told them once more how proud he was of them.

As the four boys reached the back of the auditorium, Tulip got up from a seat in the very back row. She hugged each boy with tears in her eyes.

"Thanks so much," she said simply. "I like the Black Dinosaurs."

STUDY GUIDE FOR
Ziggy and the Black Dinosaurs #6:
Stars and Sparks on Stage
BY SHARON M. DRAPER

DISCUSSION TOPICS

CHAPTER 1

1. Describe the sights, sounds, and smells of Ziggy's bath time.
2. From the conversation that Ziggy has with his mother, what can you tell about the relationship between the two?
3. Give an example of Ziggy's unusual eating habits.
4. Even though Ziggy eats unusual foods, explain how his food choices are basically healthy.
5. Describe the boys' school building and the area around it. Tell how their school is similar or different from your own.
6. What kinds of dreams do the boys have about becoming successful as singers?
7. "She'll Be Coming 'Round the Mountain" is an

old American folk song with many possible verses. Make up your own verses to it.

8. "In the distance, their gravel-covered track waited for runners, and the old wooden bleachers sat empty." Write another descriptive sentence that gives human characteristics or feelings to nonliving things.

9. Describe the singing voices of the four boys.

10. "None of them noticed the car that was parked in the tall grass behind the athletic stands." Make a prediction about how that car becomes important in the story.

CHAPTER 2

1. Describe Mr. Cavendish. What lets you know he is a good teacher?

2. What does Mr. Cavendish believe about performing?

3. What does Mr. Cavendish believe about competing for prizes?

4. Who donated the prize money and why?

5. How does Ziggy help Mimi during the tryouts?

6. Describe Bill and Tito's performance for the tryouts.

7. What song do the Black Dinosaurs sing for the tryouts?

8. What makes their song funny?

9. What would you perform if you could be in a talent show?

10. Make a prediction: What will happen when the list is posted?

CHAPTER 3

1. Why do the boys stay late with Mr. Cavendish?

2. Why does Ziggy like being in the school when it's empty?

3. How do the boys discover the new girl?

4. Describe Tulip when the boys first meet her.

5. Why does Mr. Cavendish call 911 even though Tulip is not seriously injured?

6. Why are Rico and Ziggy excited about having the responsibility of dialing 911?

7. Where do Tulip and her mother come from and why are they homeless?

8. Why do you think Jerome invites Tulip and her mother to his house?

9. How can you tell all four boys want to impress Tulip?

10. If you discovered a medical emergency at your school, what would you do?

CHAPTER 4

1. Give an example of how rumors operate in a school.

2. Compare the school when it is empty to when students fill the halls.

3. Compare how Tulip looks when the boys first meet her to how she looks the following morning.

4. What difficulties might be encountered in trying to find Tulip's school records?

5. How does Tulip shine in math class?

6. Write some additional verses to Rico's silly poem about the zoo and to Tulip's poem about the blues.

7. What does Tulip say after she finishes reciting

her poem? What was your response to her poem?

8. How does Brandy react to Tulip and why?

9. Why is poetry a good way to express feelings?

10. Make a prediction: What will the other students think of a new girl who is good at everything?

CHAPTER 5

1. How will the choir participate in the talent show?

2. How do you know Mr. Cavendish is a teacher who focuses on encouragement?

3. What is noticeable about Tulip's singing voice?

4. Why are the Black Dinosaurs worried?

5. What does Tulip say when she finishes her song?

6. What does Tulip say when she completes every task well?

7. Name several negative things about being homeless.

8. How do you think Tulip feels about being the new student at her school?

9. What do you think the other students understand about Tulip's situation?

10. Make a prediction: What will happen at the talent show?

CHAPTER 6

1. How did the boys build their clubhouse?

2. Describe the inside of their clubhouse.

3. Which of the four boys dislikes bugs? How do you know?

4. Tell how the boys could use the prize money to improve their clubhouse.

5. How does Jerome's grandmother help Tulip and her mom?

6. What do the boys think about Tulip and her skills and abilities?

7. Why do you think the boys are a little worried about their chances in the talent show?

8. What do they decide to do to improve their act?

9. Write some additional verses to "Fooba Wooba John."

10. How do you know Jerome is surprised to see Tulip?

CHAPTER 7

1. Why do you think Jerome is so nervous about having Tulip in the clubhouse?
2. What is unusual about having a girl in the clubhouse?
3. How did the club get the name the Black Dinosaurs?
4. What do you think it was like for Tulip during the hurricane?
5. What do you think the boys learn as they talk to Tulip about the hurricane?
6. What is the difference between collecting money to send to a disaster and meeting a person who was involved in the disaster?
7. Write some additional verses to "Boom Boom, Ain't It Great to Be Crazy?"
8. How do you know Jerome likes Tulip a little?
9. Why do the boys feel a little guilty about wanting to win the prize money?
10. What final plans do they make for the show?

CHAPTER 8

1. What is the difference between practicing in an empty auditorium and performing for people in the audience?
2. How do you know the boys are worried about Tulip and her singing abilities?
3. What colors would Ziggy use to paint the clubhouse?
4. What colors would you use if you had to paint a clubhouse? Tell why.
5. What do some of the children dream of buying with $200?
6. Why do you think Mrs. Powell gives the homework assignment that she does?
7. Why do you think Tulip chooses the items that she does?
8. Give examples to show that Mrs. Powell is a good teacher.
9. Write some additional verses to Ziggy's grocery store poem.
10. Make a prediction. What will happen between Tulip and Brandy?

CHAPTER 9

1. Describe the boys' practice for the talent show.

2. Describe their costumes for the show.

3. Why do you think the four boys feel confident about the show?

4. How do you know they have doubts as well?

5. Why do you think Tulip wears the same clothes every day?

6. What good things have happened in Tulip's life recently?

7. What do you learn about Simon and his early problems with reading?

8. How is Simon's situation similar to that of many other students?

9. How did Mr. Stanker help Simon and change his outlook on school and reading?

10. Practice chanting "Reader's Rap" with your class. Make up additional verses to go with the chorus.

CHAPTER 10

1. Describe the tension backstage just before the

show. Why do you think these things happen?

2. How do you think the people in the audience feel as they wait for the show to begin?

3. Give two reasons why "The Star-Spangled Banner" is a good start for the show.

4. What do you think of Brandy's poem? What do you think she is trying to say?

5. Describe Tulip's performance.

6. Describe the performance of the Black Dinosaurs.

7. From the written description, who do you think does the better job—Tulip or the Black Dinosaurs?

8. How do you think the four boys feel when they hear their name called?

9. Why do you think they choose to give the money away, even though they really want it?

10. How do you think Tulip feels about losing the competition but winning the prize?

ADDITIONAL ACTIVITIES

Use the Internet, an encyclopedia, or other books
to find out more about the following:

A. Information to explore and discover
1. Talent shows
2. Homeless people in the United States
3. Homeless shelters
4. Hurricane Katrina
5. American folk songs and spirituals
6. Learning to play an instrument
7. Learning to sing and perform on stage
8. Writing poetry
9. Building a clubhouse
10. Difficulties in learning to read

B. Vocabulary
1. Competition
2. Lyrics
3. Stanza

4. Refrain

5. Chorus

6. Donation

7. Enthusiastic

8. Poetry

9. Costume

10. Performance

C. Jobs to explore

1. Music teacher

2. Social worker

3. Homeless advocate

4. English teacher

5. Poet or songwriter

6. Musician

7. Singer

8. Emergency medical technician

9. Grocery store owner

10. Event producer

D. Investigations

1. Find out what happens in your town if someone

has no place to live. What shelters or services are available?

2-7. Investigate the following things about Hurricane Katrina:

2. What a category four or five storm is

3. The physical damage that was done

4. The damage to businesses and jobs

5. The damage to people and their lives

6. The resulting homelessness and displacement of people

7. What happened to all the pets and other animals after the storm

8-10. List all the factors that would have to be considered to have a successful talent show, including:

8. Performers, acts, tryouts, and costumes

9. Rules and regulations to make it safe, fair, and sensible

10. Costs, time, tickets, and advertisements

E. Writing activities

1. Tell the story of someone who is made homeless

by a storm or any other terrible event he or she has no control over. Draw pictures to accompany your narrative.

2. Write a story, with you as the main character, as you plan a talent show or with you as a performer.

3. Make up a story about any performer you choose, whether a real person or someone you make up. Be creative. Describe the life of that person.

4. Write an account of what it might be like to work at a homeless shelter. Include sights, sounds, and smells in your story.

5. Using any of the poems or songs in the book as a model, write a poem or song of your own.

6. Write a mystery that includes clues about a stranger in your school. At the end of your story show how the clues are solved.

7. Write a newspaper story that reports the events of the talent show at Ziggy's school. Pretend you are interviewing each performer after the show.

8. Mrs. Powell gives the students an assignment to

write an essay called "What I Would Do with Two Hundred Dollars" and to bring an ad that shows the cost of the items they choose. Do the same assignment.

9. Mr. Cavendish said, "Without music and drama and the arts, we are nothing." Write an essay that explains what you think he means. In your essay you should agree or disagree with his statement.

10. Write a poem about Tulip.

F. Organizations and their websites
(Please note: These are listed for further study and investigation and are for informational purposes only. Use with children at your discretion.)

1. Poetry for kids
   www.gigglepoetry.com
2. Poetry for kids
   www.poetry4kids.com
3. Talent shows
   en.wikipedia.org/wiki/Talent_show

4. Writing songs with children
   www.geocities.com/rainforest/vines/2400/
   writingsongs. html)
5. Basic information on Katrina
   en.wikipedia.org/wiki/Hurricane_Katrina
6. On homelessness
   www.hud.gov/homeless/index.cfm
7. On ending homelessness
   www.endhomelessness.org